# MAX and ME
## and the
# WILD WEST

# MAX and ME
## and the
# WILD WEST

**by Gery Greer and Bob Ruddick**

A Harper Trophy Book

Harper & Row, Publishers

*To*
*Virginia, Chuck,*
*Nick, and Elizabeth*

# 1

I took a deep breath. It was now or never. It was going to be tough, and it was going to be dangerous, but I was as ready as I'd ever be. I was ready to break the news to my best friend, Max Zilinski, about the favor I'd done for him.

A favor he hadn't exactly asked me to do. A favor that had to do with the girl of his dreams, Dawn Sharington.

But at least I'd picked the right time to tell him—while his mind was occupied and his hands were full. The way I figured it, this greatly reduced the chances that he'd clobber me.

"Uh, say, Max . . ." I began.

He didn't hear me. Max has terrific powers of concentration, and at the moment he was concentrating on the control panel of Professor Flybender's Fully Guaranteed One-Of-A-Kind Time Machine. We were in our clubhouse, way out among the trees in my backyard—just Max and me and the weird seven-foot-tall contraption that we'd picked up at a garage sale for $2.50. As soon as Max finished making a few last-minute adjustments, we were planning to pull the gigantic ON lever that juts out from the side of the machine. Then we'd be off on another trip through time. Next stop, the Wild West. More than one hundred years ago.

But first, the big news.

"Uh, say, Max . . ." I said again, a little louder this time.

"Um?" He didn't even glance up. His eyes were glued to the Dial-a-Date control as he carefully turned the knobs to read A.D. 1882.

"I ran into Dawn Sharington today," I said casually.

Max froze, one hand on a knob and the other hand about to push his glasses back up on his nose.

"Dawn Sharington?" he asked.

I think he was trying to sound relaxed and natural, but his voice came out sort of funny. Sort of like a croak. Maybe like a big bullfrog might sound if you suddenly whispered the name of his true love in his ear.

Of course, Max would never admit that Dawn is his true love. I mean, he's never even come right out and said he likes her or anything. But I have ways of knowing. Mainly, I've observed that whenever he's around her he turns bright red, peeks at her out of the corner of his eye, bumps into things a lot, and replies to everything you say to him with, "Uh . . . sure . . . uh . . . huh?"

"Yeah, Dawn Sharington," I said cheerfully. "She's having a party at her house for the girls' softball team tonight, and she was wondering how she was going to entertain all those girls. So naturally, I thought of you."

A look of panic swept over Max's face. *"Me?"*

"Right. I volunteered you to do a magic show."

Max went white.

I hurried on. "I told her all about how you're taking a correspondence course called 'How to Be a Magician.' And by the way, I thought of a great name for you, too: Max the Magnificent. Dawn says it sounds really cute. She says she can hardly wait."

Max gave an outraged sputter and reached for me with both hands, so I took the precaution of ducking around to the back side of the time machine. There are times, during a conversation, when it can be a good thing to keep something large between you and the other party.

And this was one of those times. Max came barreling around the time machine and made a diving grab for me. I dodged, keeping the machine between us.

"Take it easy, Max," I said, peeking around at him. "What're you worried about? You're a terrific magician. Believe me, they're going to love you. *Dawn's* going to love you."

"Oh, sure," groaned Max. He gave up the chase and flopped down on our old rumpled cot. Gloomily he stared up at the ceiling. "I've never given a magic show in my life. Max the *Magnificent!* I'll make a magnificent *fool* of myself." He closed his eyes and shuddered. "They'll all laugh their heads off."

That was Max for you—the old Worry Wart himself. Actually, although he'd only been taking this correspondence course from the American College of Magic and Illusion for four months, he was already a really good magician. I should know. Every time he got a new trick in the mail, he'd head over to our clubhouse and drive me crazy by practicing it over and over until he got it right. Max isn't the sort of person who does things halfway.

And that includes worrying.

I came out from behind the time machine and stood in front of the cot with my hands on my hips.

"What you need, Max," I announced firmly, "is more self-confidence. You've got to think positive. You've got to believe in yourself. You've got to take the bull by the horns, think big, and put your best foot forward."

I kind of liked the sound of this advice, but it didn't make much of an impression on the Worry Wart. "If I put my best foot forward," he muttered glumly, "I'll probably trip over the carpet."

I shifted my tactics. "Look," I said, "you already know about a hundred tricks—"

"Twenty-two," Max grumbled. He's very big on accuracy.

"—which is more than you could use in one magic show anyway. So just pick your ten best and you'll be great."

"Hmmpf," said Max, but I could tell I was softening him up by the way he started nibbling on his thumbnail. He always does that when he's busy sorting something out in his mind. Which is often. More than anyone else I know, Max is a thinker. Whenever he runs into a problem, he just plain *thinks* it to death—taking his time, studying it from every possible angle, making mental lists of every possible solution. I call him Motor-Mind.

I let some time pass. Convincing Max to do something is sort of like fishing—it requires a lot of patience. Finally, I threw out a little more bait. "You could start with your Banana Split trick," I suggested.

"Yeah . . ." said Max, nodding thoughtfully. "I suppose I *might* get through that one without flubbing it up. . . ."

"And at the end of the show," I offered, "for your grand finale, you could do the one where you disappear in a puff of smoke."

Max sat up. "Hmmm. Not bad," he admitted. "It's simple, but it's effective. Of course, it's really a two-man trick. It's better if one person sets off the smoke bomb while the other person distracts the audience."

"No problem," I said. "I already told Dawn I was going to be your trusty assistant. From now on just call me Steve the Stupendous."

"Oh, wonderful," said Max dryly. "We'll make a great team. One magnificent fool and one stupendous fool." But I could tell he was glad he'd have some help. He began to look almost cheerful.

"Well!" I said, rubbing my hands together and turning my attention to the time machine. "Now that that's settled, we can get on with more important business—our trip to 'those thrilling days of yesteryear.' Just think: stagecoaches, cattle drives, shootouts!"

I started humming the theme from *The Lone Ranger*.

"We can't go," said Max.

I stopped humming. *"What?"*

"We can't go," he repeated, looking stubborn. He pushed his glasses firmly back up on his nose. "If Dawn's party's tonight, there's not much time for me to practice, and I'll need all the practice I can get."

"Of course you will," I said, catching him off guard. It always catches Max off guard when I agree with him. "But haven't you forgotten something? Haven't you forgotten how this fantastic piece of machinery works?"

I gave the time machine an affectionate pat and a knob fell off. It clattered to the floor and bounced under the cot.

"What are you talking about?" said Max, leaning over to peer under the cot. He reached down, fished around for a few seconds, and found the knob.

"Just this," I said crisply. "We're planning to stay in the Wild West for two days, right?"

Max nodded. He'd already set the Length-of-Stay control for "002 Days." "So?" he asked. He got up and carefully replaced the knob.

"So after two days, the time machine will automatically return us to the present. And no time will have passed here, right? We'll arrive back exactly when we left."

"Yes, but—"

"Which means," I concluded grandly, "that you'll have two whole days to practice your magic tricks while we're in the Wild West, and then when we come back, you'll still have the rest of today to put the final polish on them! How's that sound?"

Max raised his eyebrows. "You're right," he said slowly. He paused and then added, "But I wouldn't be able to take any of my magic equipment with me into the past."

A good point. There was no way to take anything solid along with us. In fact, we wouldn't even be able to take our own *bodies* with us. The only other time we'd used the time machine—when we went on a three-day jaunt to England during the Middle Ages —we'd been transported into the bodies of people who were already living at that time. Or rather, in Max's case, the body of a *horse* who was already living at that time. I became a famous knight, and Max arrived as my horse.

Actually, now that I thought about it, I realized that if Max happened to materialize as some sort of animal again, he was going to have a very difficult time practicing any magic tricks, even if he did have equipment. But I decided not to bring that up. Some things are better left undiscussed.

"You won't need any equipment," I assured him. "While we're in the Wild West, you can practice the tricks that don't need any special props—like your mind-reading trick, and plucking coins from behind people's ears, and stuff like that. Then when we get back to the present, you can practice your other tricks. Just think," I added temptingly. *"Two whole days."*

"Well . . ." said Max, mulling it over, ". . . I suppose I *might*—"

"Great! That's it then," I said, giving him a hearty

whack on the back. "Now, let's get this show on the road."

I reached for the ON lever.

"Wait!" said Max, grabbing my arm. "I haven't set the Pick-a-Place control yet."

"Oh. Right." I stepped aside so he could make the final adjustment. Max loves tinkering with machines, so naturally he was chief-in-charge of making sure everything was shipshape and ready to go.

He took his job seriously, too. Eyebrows drawn together in concentration, he peered at the tiny map of the world that was pinned under glass on the front of the time machine. Then, using two knobs, he maneuvered a red dot across the face of the map until the dot was over the American West, just about in the middle of where the Arizona Territory would be.

"That should do it," said Max, standing back and polishing his glasses on his shirttail. He gazed admiringly at the time machine. "Boy, that Professor Flybender must have been a real genius."

I had to agree with him there. Of course, we'd never actually met Professor Flybender. All we knew about him was that he was this strange, secretive inventor who'd lived in Flat Rock before Max or I moved here. Suddenly, about eight years ago, he announced that he'd figured out where the lost continent of Atlantis was and that he was going on a one-man expedition to find it. He never came back, and no one's heard from him since.

After a few years the professor's house was sold to pay off his debts, and a guy named Mr. Cooper bought it, furniture and all. Lucky for us, Mr. Cooper doesn't like clutter. Early this summer he decided to have a garage sale, and among the things he dragged down from the attic and put on sale was the time machine, packed in a crate marked: MAINLY, ONE GENUINE, COMPLETELY AUTOMATED, EASILY ASSEMBLED, ONE-OF-A-KIND TIME MACHINE! FULLY GUARANTEED!

Of course, Mr. Cooper didn't believe for a minute it was a real time machine or he never would've sold it to Max and me. Especially for the bargain price of $2.50.

"I'll say this," said Max, still admiring the time machine. "It's got style."

"Gobs of it," I agreed.

We hadn't always thought so. When we'd first gotten it, before we had a chance to see if it worked, Max had called it "Flybender's Fantastic Hunk of Junk." But that was because it took some getting used to. I mean, it definitely didn't look like one of your standard, high-tech, computerized pieces of hardware.

In the first place, there was this huge fan mounted right on top, like a propeller on a beanie cap. In the second place, there was that oversized ON-OFF lever that stuck out from the side like a huge arm waving a friendly hello. And finally, there were all those colored lights surrounding all those old-fashioned meters and dials and switches and things.

All in all, Flybender's time machine looked like something that would be right at home in one of those old low-budget science-fiction movies where everybody carries plastic ray guns and the hero says things like, "I don't like the looks of that spaceship, Chip! Look! It's got teeth!"

"So," I said to Max, "are we ready to go?"

"All set," he said.

We took up our positions, standing side by side in front of the time machine. I grasped the ON lever and was just about to throw my weight against it when Max suddenly held up his hand.

"Hold it!" he said, looking worried. "I just thought of something."

I let go of the lever. "What now?" I sighed.

"This magic show tonight. What am I going to wear for a magician's costume?"

"Max, will you forget about the magic show? We're about to go to the Wild West here. You know, Boot Hill, Indian scouts, get out of town before sunset. Things like that."

"Yeah, I know, but I don't have anything to wear for the magic show," he persisted. "I mean, a magician's supposed to dress up in a black cape or a tuxedo or something, but I don't have any of that stuff. Aren't I going to look pretty stupid just wearing ordinary, everyday clothes?"

The Worry Wart rides again, I thought.

Suddenly an idea popped into my head. It was the wrong time to joke, but I couldn't resist. "Oh, didn't I tell you, Max?" I said innocently. "Dawn said the party's going to be a slumber party, so I promised her you'd get into the spirit of things by wearing your pajamas."

Max stopped breathing and his eyes bugged out. For a second there I thought he was going to keel

10

over in a dead faint. I figured I'd better say something.

"Just kidding," I said cheerily.

Slowly, Max returned to the world of the living. The color came back into his cheeks, and he glared at me like a tiger sizing up its next meal. He was going to jump me for sure, but I didn't give him the chance. I seized the huge lever and, mustering all my strength, pulled it down to ON.

Professor Flybender's time machine rumbled into action.

# 2

The time machine's lights flickered on, blazed bright, and began to flash in crazy, swirling patterns. There was a buzzing sound, and then a hissing. Sparks flew. Jets of steam spurted from seams along the sides of the machine. Needles on gauges danced uncertainly back and forth and then pinned themselves at the far ends of the scales.

Then came the wailing sound. From somewhere deep inside the machine, it began low and weird and then grew higher, louder, and weirder—like the angry screech of something hairy and horrible.

The huge fan on top began to turn. Gathering speed, its giant blades whipped the air faster and faster. The clubhouse began to shake. Our bookcase fell over, landing with a crash, the books sprawling. The floor was vibrating violently, and I lost my footing and stumbled backward against the wall. Bracing myself with one hand, I held my other hand out in front of my face—and watched as it dissolved into a million tiny dots of color, fading fast.

And then darkness.

A whistling, howling wind raged about me as I felt myself tumbling end over end through a pitch-black void. Upward? Downward? I didn't know. Whirling, cartwheeling, I felt like a speck of dust being sucked into a powerful vacuum cleaner.

Suddenly the wind stopped, and in that same instant I landed with a heavy thump.

I had arrived.

Or at least I was pretty sure I'd arrived. I couldn't see anything, but I could hear a sound: a creaking, rattling sound, and somewhere behind it, a clackety-clack, clackety-clack.

Then all at once I could see: a window, and through the window a broad, sunlit landscape of sage-brush, cactus, red-rock buttes, and distant mesas. The whole landscape was slowly moving by.

I glanced around me.

I was on a train!

The Wild West! I thought excitedly. Flybender's Fully Guaranteed Time Machine had done it again!

Eagerly I took a closer look at my surroundings.

One thing was for sure, this was no ordinary train car. Everything was luxurious and expensive-looking—with red velvet seats, fancy curtains at the windows, polished brass lamps, and stylish brass hat racks. There was even a shelf with small leather-bound books on one wall and a large gold-framed mirror on the other.

I was obviously traveling first class, whoever I was.

And now that I thought about it, *who was I?*

I glanced down at myself. Cowboy boots, black pants, white shirt, and a pearl-gray vest with a silver watch chain draped across it. So far, so good. Also, as far as I could tell, I seemed to be lean and athletic, and judging from the long legs stretching out in front of me, at least six feet tall. No guns. Well, that was okay. I was probably deadly with my bare hands alone.

Somebody was staring at me.

It was the guy sitting in the opposite seat, facing me. In fact, he seemed to be the only other person in the car, which meant that I was probably supposed to know him. Maybe we were traveling together or something.

I sized him up. He was in his mid-twenties, I figured, and had a boyish face with bright, intelligent eyes. For some reason he looked out of place here in the rugged West. Maybe it was because of his carefully pressed brown suit with matching vest, or his shiny brown shoes, or that newspaper folded neatly over one knee. I mean, this guy was definitely no cowpoke. Here was an eastern city-slicker if I ever saw one.

He was studying me intently, a peculiar expression on his face.

Maybe it was Max, trying to figure out if this was me. But then again, maybe it wasn't Max. Maybe it was just some guy trying to figure out why I was acting so strange.

Well, when in doubt, plunge right in.

"Max?" I ventured, my voice coming out deep and smooth. "That you?"

"Steve!" he said, his face relaxing into a big grin.

"I *thought* that might be you." Then he snickered.

And then he snickered again.

Hmmm. What was so funny?

Now he chuckled, still eyeing me. I began to get an uneasy feeling.

"All right, Max," I demanded. "What gives?"

"Oh, nothing," he said, beginning to chortle so hard he could barely talk. "Don't worry about it. It's just your . . . it's just your . . ."

"It's just my *what?*"

He gave a horselaugh. "It's just your h—"

Suddenly, there was a loud commotion coming from the car ahead of us. It was a struggle of some kind—with shouting voices, a crash, the sound of scuffling feet.

A few seconds later the door to our car burst open, and in charged a train conductor, in a blue uniform, dragging a struggling man by the arm.

"Unhand me, you big moose!" the man was protesting loudly. His flashy green jacket had been pulled off one shoulder, his black-and-white checkered vest had popped a couple of buttons, and his black bow tie was tilted at a steep angle. In his free hand he was clutching a derby hat. He whacked the conductor a couple of times with the hat. "My lawyers will hear about this!"

The conductor didn't seem impressed. "Save it for the judge, Wilbur," he said.

He hauled his prisoner down the aisle. I figured he was taking him to the rear of the train to lock him up somewhere, but just as the two of them came alongside Max and me, the conductor stopped abruptly.

He seized his prisoner by the back of his shirt collar and thrust him forward for my inspection. I sat back, startled.

"I done tracked him down, Mr. Langsfield," the conductor informed me respectfully. "I searched this here train from one end to the other, and where do you reckon I finally found the low-down sneakin' rattlesnake? Hidin' on top of the baggage car!"

"I was not!" declared the man in the checkered vest indignantly. He had a round face with a long nose and wore his short brown hair parted down the middle. "I most certainly was *not* hiding! I was on top of that baggage car, gentlemen, for one reason and one reason only. I was taking the sun. Following my doctor's orders to the letter, I might add. I'm not well, you know." He carefully removed a handkerchief from his coat pocket and coughed softly into it.

The conductor gave a loud snort. "Think we was born yesterday?" he demanded. Then he turned back to me and said, "I'm sure you'll be wantin' to press charges, sir, after what this here varmint done to you."

I blinked. "Huh?"

"I said I'm sure you'll be wantin' to press charges against this here varmint."

"Well, uh, that depends . . ." I stammered.

It depended on what this here varmint had done to me. Or rather, this guy. I checked myself over. I was pretty sure he hadn't shot me. I mean, it'd be kind of hard not to notice a thing like that. Besides, he didn't look like the violent type. But that still left a lot of possibilities. He could've picked my pocket,

16

for instance, or cheated me at cards, or swindled me out of a gold mine, or—

"I believe I can explain this little misunderstanding," piped up the prisoner.

Great, I thought. Now we were getting somewhere.

"Oh?" I said encouragingly.

"Yes, indeed, Mr. Langsfield," said Wilbur. "I believe I can ease your mind and put this matter to rest in a mere jiffy. A mere minute or two of your time. A mere—"

"The point, Wilbur," said the conductor gruffly. "Get to the point."

"Absolutely," said Wilbur. "Certainly. I'd be happy to. I know you're a busy man, Mr. Langsfield, so naturally I'll try to be as brief as humanly possible." He straightened his bow tie. "I simply want to say that this matter of your hair was an accident. An unfortunate accident and a deeply regrettable one, but an accident nonetheless."

I stared at him.

"My *what?*" I said.

"Your hair," said Wilbur.

I heard a snicker coming from Max's direction.

I looked at the conductor. Then at Wilbur. Then at Max. They were all looking at my hair.

Uh-oh, I thought.

# 3

Slowly I raised my hands to my hair and carefully felt all over.

This was not good.

My hair had a stiff, sticky, tar-like feel to it, sort of like the feeling of an asphalt highway in the hot sun. Also, most of it seemed to be sticking straight out all around the front, sides, and back, like the brim of a huge hat. When I pulled down on it and let it go, it made a twanging sound.

Max cackled.

I turned to Wilbur and aimed a stern, accusing glare at him.

"Actually," Wilbur said hastily, "most folks don't realize that the manufacture of hair tonic is an extremely complicated and very delicate business. Add just a little too much rose water or whale oil or varnish and you can spoil the whole batch."

"Varnish!" I exploded.

"But don't you worry, Mr. Langsfield," he hurried on. "If you're not entirely satisfied with the results, you're entitled to a full and complete refund. Like it says on each and every bottle of Wilbur's Why-Not-Be-Handsome Hair Tonic: 'This product is one hundred percent guaranteed.' "

"Guaranteed to make a feller look like a blamed, durned fool!" burst out the conductor. "Why, if I saw a feller walkin' down the street like this—with his hair a-stickin' out all stiff like the wings of a big old black bat—I'd think he was some kind of rip-snortin' jackass without no brains at all! Why, I never seen such a—"

The conductor suddenly noticed me eyeing him and stopped short. He coughed nervously. " 'Course, you'll pardon me fer sayin' so, sir," he said politely.

Max cackled again. "No need to apologize," he assured the conductor. "We're all men of the world here, and I think we know a ripsnortin' jackass when we see one."

If I'd had a pencil and paper handy, I'd have made a note to myself: "Put this Max Zilinski character out of his misery at the first opportunity."

Just then the train whistle blew: two short toots followed by a long, lingering blast. The conductor pulled out a pocket watch, checked the time, and then—still with a good grip on Wilbur's collar—leaned over and squinted out the window. We were chugging along the base of a high mesa.

"Next stop, Silver Gulch," he announced. "The richest, roughest boomtown in the West." He straightened up again. "It's been an honor havin' you and yer newspaper friend, Mr. Huff, aboard," he said, nodding at Max and me. So Max was a newspaperman! "And don't you worry none about yer baggage. It'll be on the platform waitin' fer you."

What? We were getting off? Max and I glanced at each other uncertainly and then stood up.

"I'll be needin' to know what you want done with this here scoundrel," the conductor continued, giving Wilbur a little shake. "I'll be happy to turn him over to the sheriff in Silver Gulch if yer a mind to press charges."

"No need for that, I'm sure," Wilbur said to me hurriedly. "Why, if you'll just wash that hair of yours with a little paint thinner, it'll be like silk by morning." He straightened his checkered vest, smoothed his hair down with both hands, and generally tried to look respectable.

I thought it over. All in all, Wilbur didn't seem like such a bad guy. In fact, he seemed . . . well, almost sort of *likable*. Sort of like a cocker spaniel, maybe. With its hair parted down the middle, of course.

And I just couldn't picture myself having a cocker spaniel thrown in the clink.

"I'm probably making a big mistake," I told the conductor, "but I guess I'll let Wilbur off the hook this time." I gave Wilbur a hard look. "*This* time," I added.

Wilbur immediately stuck out his hand for me to shake. "Mr. Langsfield," he said emotionally, "you have just earned the undying gratitude of Wilbur J. McNabb."

I shook his hand. What else could I do?

"And believe me," he went on, "a McNabb knows the meaning of the word 'gratitude.' It's just like what

20

folks say about me all the way from San Francisco to Amarillo. They say—"

"They probably say he can talk the ears off a jackrabbit," said the conductor, sighing loudly. He let go of Wilbur's collar and started up the aisle. "Well, if you gents'll excuse me, I reckon I'd best see to the baggage."

The train was slowing down. We passed a shack with a horse corral near it.

"Oh, conductor," Wilbur called cheerfully after him. "I believe I'll have a look around Silver Gulch myself. Would you mind putting my bag off, too?"

"With pleasure," muttered the conductor, slamming the door behind him.

Max and I headed for the rear door, with Wilbur tagging along after us.

"I found that conductor to be a rather ill-tempered individual, didn't you?" Wilbur remarked. "I wonder if his shoes are too tight."

I hardly heard him. On the wall to the left, in the large mirror with the fancy gold frame, I'd just caught a glimpse of myself.

I stopped dead in my tracks and stared in horrified fascination.

Actually, I suppose you could say it was one of those good-news–bad-news situations. The good news was that—from the forehead down—I was a very good-looking guy, in an interesting sort of way. I was about twenty-five years old, and although I didn't look tough like a gunfighter or anything, I did have this strange, intense look. My jaw was strong, my nose was straight, and my eyes were deep set and dark blue. And of course, the scar helped, too—the one on my left cheekbone, back near my ear. It was faint, about two inches long, and added nicely to the overall dashing effect.

That was the good news. The bad news was— you guessed it—my hair. There it was, sticking out stiff and shiny all around the sides of my head, like a big black plastic Frisbee. Just looking at it made me realize something. It made me realize that until that moment, I had never truly known what a rip-snortin' jackass looked like.

"Hey, look at all those people out there!" said Max, peering out the window. We were pulling slowly into the station. "Looks like the whole town's out there waiting for the train."

I glanced outside. He was right. There must have been four or five hundred people on the platform, just sort of milling around. I gave a quiet groan. Unless I was very much mistaken, I was about to become the laughingstock of the richest, roughest boomtown in the West.

"I could let you borrow my hat," volunteered Wilbur, reading my mind.

"Your hat?" I eyed Wilbur's derby. It looked pretty small, but if I pulled it down far enough, it just might get me by. Of course, my hair would still be sticking out under the brim, but with luck nobody would notice. Besides, I was in no position to be picky.

"Thanks, Wilbur," I said.

As the three of us started toward the door, I crammed Wilbur's hat on my head, pulled it down as far as it would go, and said a silent prayer that I'd be able to slip into town unnoticed.

A moment later, we stepped off the train and onto the crowded platform.

No sooner had my feet hit the ground than a tough-looking woman in a brown slouch hat, jeans with suspenders, and a rough brown shirt with rolled-up sleeves gave a loud yell and pointed straight at me.

"It's him! It's Desmond Langsfield hisself!" she bellowed. "Strike up the band, boys!"

# 4

The woman in the slouch hat came charging toward me, grinning eagerly. The rest of the crowd was surging my way, too, but she definitely had the jump on them. Somewhere in the background a brass band began to belt out a quick-paced marching song, slightly off-key.

Braking to a stop in front of me, the woman seized my hand and gave me a bone-crushing handshake that almost brought me to my knees.

"Well, danged if it ain't a pleasure to meet you, Mr. Langsfield," she said, pumping my hand energetically, "and welcome to Silver Gulch! The name's Nellamint Bradshaw, but you kin jest call me Nellie."

She let go of my hand and gave me a friendly wallop on the shoulder that moved me sideways about a foot.

"I'm president of the Silver Gulch Cultur'l Committee," she went on, shoving up her sleeves, "and that's how come I'm here to meet you. Now, if you'll jest step this way, the speaker's platform's right over yonder. The folks'll be expectin' you to say a few words."

Before I could open my mouth to protest, she took hold of my arm and began propelling me through the crowd toward a big wooden freight wagon parked in front of the station door.

"Outta the way, you galoots!" she barked, clearing a path. "Mr. Langsfield's gonna make a speech!"

A *speech?* How was I going to make a speech when I didn't have the foggiest idea who I was or why I was there? I looked around desperately for Max. Usually old Motor-Mind is good for a brilliant idea or two whenever I'm in a tight spot, but I couldn't find him anywhere among all the eager faces around me. Wilbur, on the other hand, was right there, marching along proudly at my side, waving grandly to one and all.

We were almost to the freight wagon when a tall, thin man stepped out of the crowd. He had a thick black mustache, shrewd gray eyes, and a pair of very large guns strapped to his sides. A silver star was pinned to his black vest.

"This here's the sheriff," Nellie said, by way of introduction. "Sheriff Clay Parker."

At the mention of the word "sheriff," Wilbur banked sharply to the left, dived into the crowd, and disappeared from view.

"Howdy," I said to the sheriff. It was all I could think of to say.

He sized me up slowly through narrowed eyes and then gave me a solemn handshake. "Howdy," he said.

I assumed that was the end of the conversation, but just before he let go of my hand, the sheriff leaned forward slightly, and in a low voice no one else could hear, said: *"The duck hasn't quacked."*

I stared at him.

"I beg your pardon?" I said.

*"The duck hasn't quacked,"* he repeated.

I *thought* that's what he'd said.

I stared at him some more. Either this sheriff was a certified Looney Tune or else he was trying to tell me something in code. But if it was a code, what did it mean?

He was obviously waiting for me to respond.

I narrowed my eyes meaningfully. "Sooner or later," I told him in a low voice, *"every* duck quacks."

He nodded, and I could see from his keen gray eyes that he agreed completely.

Yep, I told myself, he's crackers. The poor guy's almost certainly crackers.

"Up here!" called Nellie. She was already standing on top of the wagon and was gesturing like mad for me to join her. "Folks is waitin'!"

I gulped, my mind racing. How was I going to get out of this? *Where was Max?* Reluctantly I put one foot on a wheel spoke and hoisted myself onto the wagon.

The band stopped playing and the crowd grew quiet.

"Ladies and gents!" boomed Nellie, her thumbs hooked in her suspenders. "This here's the feller you all been hearin' about! Right here, in the flesh, the famous Mr. Desmond Langsfield hisself! Give him a big hand!"

With that, she jumped down off the wagon.

I was alone.

And as the crowd cheered and clapped and whistled, I stood there dumbly, a sickly smile frozen on my face, my knees turning to sponges.

I wonder, I thought with rising panic, if they've heard the one about the hippopotamus with the pink tennis shoes.

"Pssst! Steve!" hissed a voice behind me.

I looked around and there was my traveling companion from the train, Mr. Huff, standing behind the wagon in his neat brown suit. It took me a second to realize it was Max.

Quickly I knelt down. "Max, where've you been?" I whispered. "I'm about to make a speech here and I don't even know who I am!"

"No problem," he whispered back, crisp and businesslike. "*I* know who you are. You're an actor. Here, read this." He handed a piece of paper up to me. "I found it in my coat pocket."

I took the paper and read it rapidly. It was a newspaper clipping.

## FAMOUS ACTOR TOURS WEST

### by Ed Huff

The illustrious star of the San Francisco stage, Desmond Langsfield, continued his tour of the West last night with a smash appearance at the Verity Theater in the Arizona mining town of Last Bonanza. An audience of more than five hundred citizens saw the actor give a magnificent one-man performance that included skits entitled *Hurricane Jake and the Rattlesnake, One Night in a Bar Room,* and *Death on the Prairie.* In addition, Mr. Langsfield recited several well-known poems, and . . .

That was all I had time to read. The applause had died away and everybody was waiting for me to give my big speech. Tucking the clipping into my vest pocket, I stood up and faced the crowd.

So I'm an actor! I thought. A famous actor, on a tour of the West! And this guy Ed Huff—alias Max—is probably traveling around with me so he can write newspaper articles about my performances. In fact, he's probably—

"Hey, mister! You just gonna stand there like a mule, or you gonna make a speech?"

I looked down. It was a kid. Right there in front of the crowd was this tough-looking, redheaded kid about twelve or thirteen years old. Just about my age, in fact, back in the present. He had his arms folded across his chest, and he looked very annoyed with me. As soon as he caught my eye, he crossed his eyes and lolled his tongue out of the corner of his mouth.

"Junior Sitwell!" yelled Nellie, leaning around several people to shake her finger at him. "You mind yer manners or I'll come over thar and learn you good!"

The kid uncrossed his eyes and pulled his tongue back into his mouth. He jammed his hands in his pockets and fixed me with a sullen glare.

Trying to ignore him, I straightened my shoul-

28

ders and prepared to address the crowd. I still didn't have any idea what I was going to say, but I did know it was going to be *short*. Very likely the shortest speech in the history of the Arizona Territory.

"Ladies and gentlemen," I began in a powerful, impressive voice, "it is indeed an honor and a privilege . . ."

I could tell out of the corner of my eye that the kid was up to something. He had something in his hand.

". . . to be here in Silver Gulch . . ."

Now he was holding it up to his mouth.

". . . on this fine sunny day . . ."

I sneaked a peek down at him. Too late I realized he had a peashooter. SPLAT! I took a spitball in the middle of my forehead.

Nobody noticed.

". . . to, uh, share with you a few thoughts . . ." I continued, removing the spitball. I decided I should have a word or two with this kid if I ever managed to corner him in a dark alley.

". . . to, uh, share with you a few thoughts . . ."

Wait, I thought. Hadn't I said that before?

". . . about, uh, some matters of general interest—"

*"The stage has been robbed!"*

The cry came from somewhere on the other side of the station, along with the thunder of approaching hoofbeats. Seconds later a rider burst into view around the side of the station, waving his hat over his head, his horse kicking up bits of dirt behind him. The rider pulled up sharply at the edge of the crowd.

*"The stage has been robbed! It's comin' in now!"*

As fascinating as my speech was, it was no match for this news. The whole crowd stampeded to the front of the station. Which was okay by me. I jumped down from the freight wagon, and Max and I stampeded along with them. We were just in time to see the stagecoach come careening around a far corner. It hurtled down the main street toward us, the horses at a furious gallop, and was reined to a stop in front of the train station, the foot brake screeching, dust swirling.

"He done it again!" exploded the driver, throwing down the reins in disgust. "Took us by surprise, so's we didn't have no warnin'!"

Sheriff Parker, who had made his way calmly to the front of the crowd, was squinting up at the driver.

"Was it Hooten?" he asked grimly.

"Yer darn tootin' it was Hooten!" wheezed the driver. "He come outta nowheres. Jumped us back at Sweetwater Gap, him and that pal of his that wears a flour sack over his head. Took the strongbox and left *that*." He leaned around and pointed to a large piece of greasy yellow paper that was stuck to the door of the stagecoach with the biggest hunting knife I'd ever seen.

On the paper, scrawled in large black letters, was a poem:

I robbed, I robbed, I robbed the stage!
Without a shot
I stole the lot!
I robbed, I robbed, I robbed the stage!

I took the gold
I'm brave and bold!
                    Gentleman John Hooten
        The Rhyming Robber of the Rockies


Nellie Bradshaw, standing nearby, gave a loud sigh. "That Gentleman John may be nothin' but a low-down polecat of an outlaw," she said, shaking her head in wonder, "but he sure do have a way with words!"

"Excuse me, Miss Bradshaw," said Max politely, "but does this Gentleman John always leave a poem when he robs a stage?"

"You bet," she said. "And it's always a humdinger, too."

I was about to ask a polite question myself. I was about to ask how come this Hooten guy could call himself "The Rhyming Robber of the Rockies" when the Rocky Mountains were hundreds of miles away. But just as I opened my mouth to speak, Sheriff Parker suddenly appeared at my side.

"My office. Three o'clock," he said in a low, urgent voice. "And be sure to use the back way."

I looked at him in astonishment, but already he was moving away, chewing one corner of his mustache, pretending he hadn't even seen me.

# 5

"The show begins at nine o'clock tonight," Nellie told
me, dusting off her slouch hat by whacking it against
her leg, "and yer the main attraction, Mr. Langsfield."

"Looking forward to it," I lied.

The crowd had broken up and Nellie was con-
ducting Max and me to our hotel. We were walking
along the boardwalk on one side of the main street,
and one thing had become pretty clear—Silver Gulch
was booming, all right. The whole town had an air
of excitement, as if everyone expected to strike it rich
by sundown, or maybe sooner. Out in the wide, dusty
street, all kinds of horse traffic was on the move: lone
riders, buckboards, buggies, and supply wagons. A
dog barked at the heels of a couple of prospectors
who were leading a pack mule and three donkeys
piled high with supplies. Both sides of the street were
lined with wooden buildings that looked as if they'd
been thrown up in a hurry, and mostly left unpainted.
Over next to the bank, a man on a ladder was ham-

mering up a sign that said, "Picks, Shovels, and Real Good Grub—Cheap."

The smell of chili and strong coffee drifted out from the Horseshoe Café as we passed. From behind the swinging doors of the Silver Palace Saloon came loud laughter, the jingle of spurs, and the slap of cards. A little farther on, out in front of Latimer's General Merchandise, we dodged around several men who were loading sacks of flour into a wagon, and a woman who was buying pickles out of a barrel. From somewhere across the street came the plinking of a piano.

"And don't you worry none about gittin' shot," Nellie went on. "Long as I'm the owner of the Last Chance Theater, there ain't no performer gonna git shot."

"Did you say *'shot'*?" I asked her. I was seriously hoping I had heard her wrong.

"Yep. But rest easy, Mr. Langsfield. Yer audience is gonna be a rough lot—and a mite high-spirited, too—but they ain't gonna be armed. I make 'em check their irons at the door."

"Good thinking," said Max.

"You bet it is," I agreed heartily. "No use having a bunch of irons floating around where someone might get hurt."

" 'Course," added Nellie, "things kin still git outta hand. 'Bout a week ago the boys took a dislikin' to a coupla song-and-dance fellers. Roughed 'em up a bit and then left 'em danglin' by their feet from the chandeliers."

I thought that over for a moment. Then I gave

a cough, trying to make it sound as sickly and asthmatic and tubercular as possible. "I think I may be coming down with something," I said feebly.

Nellie didn't hear me. She'd come to a stop and was pointing across the street. "Yonder's the Last Chance," she said proudly.

Max and I looked. Towering over a blacksmith shop on one side and an assay office on the other was a large two-story wooden building with a high false front rising above it. Across the false front, in big black letters, was painted THE LAST CHANCE THEATER. Underneath, in smaller letters, it said, *Plays, Variety Acts, and Better Type Shows*. And underneath that, in even smaller letters, *Nellie Bradshaw, Owner and Proprietress*.

"It ain't fancy, but it's built solid," Nellie told us.

"It looks great," said Max admiringly. "How long have you been in the theater business?"

"Jest a coupla months. Fact is, I'm a stage driver by trade. Drove fer Southwest Stagecoach Lines fer pretty near fifteen years."

"You were a *stagecoach driver?*" I said, surprised.

"Yep. But I gave it up. A wheel come off over by Thunder Pass and I got throwed into a gully. Laid me up fer quite a spell, and that's when I decided to go into a safer line of work, so I took up prospectin'."

Max and I just stared at her. This, I thought to myself, was the kind of speaker our school ought to bring in on Career Day.

"No more'n six days later," she went on, "over

west of here 'bout a mile and a quarter, I come on to the biggest, thickest, prettiest vein of silver you ever seen. Named it the Big Surprise. Pays real good."

"You mean you actually own a silver mine?" asked Max.

"Sure do. 'Course, it warn't nothin' but luck that I come on to the vein in the first place, so I figure it's only fittin' fer me to share my good fortune with the folks of Silver Gulch. First thing I done was have a schoolhouse built fer the town young'uns. Then I built this here theater and commenced bringin' in culture. Don't mean to say nothin' against nobody, but the truth is, they's a heap of galoots around here what kin use all the culture they kin git."

I glanced around me, and yes, I did see one or two galoots of the sort Nellie might have been referring to. One of them—a lean, wiry man with a tied-down gun and quick, furtive movements—shoved past me on the boardwalk. His lank blond hair was shoulder-length, his face was unshaven, and he had wild, killer eyes. Unless I missed my guess, he definitely hadn't attended as many concerts and lectures and discussion groups as he should have.

Nellie was on the move again. "Thisaway," she said. She led us down to the Gulch Hotel, which was about a block farther on, and introduced us to the man at the desk. Then she got us the keys to our rooms and explained that our trunks were being brought from the station and would be delivered shortly. Finally, she excused herself, saying she had a "fearsome lot of chores" to do before that night's performance.

"Be seein' you gents later," she said. She hitched up her jeans and went striding out the door, her boots making solid clomping sounds on the boardwalk outside.

Right away, I took Max aside.

"I've got a little chore of my own to do," I said. "I spotted a barbershop down that first side street we passed."

"Oh, right," said Max, snickering. "I'd almost forgotten about your hair. Actually, it doesn't look half bad under your hat."

"Yeah, but I can't wear a hat all the time. The sooner I get to that barbershop the better. Are you coming?"

"Wouldn't miss it," said Max, following me out the door. "After all, the barber may have to soften up your hair with a sledgehammer, and he might need me to hold you down."

# 6

Mr. Otto Stringfellow, barber, walked slowly around me as I sat leaning back in his big wooden barber's chair, my head on the headrest, a white towel around my neck. From deep in his throat came a sort of chuffing sound, like a steam locomotive struggling uphill. This chuffing sound, I had already learned, meant that Mr. Stringfellow was once again trying to suppress a laugh.

"Now this here has got my professional curiosity up," he said, chuffing away. "It isn't often I get a case of genuine cast-iron hair."

"Do you think you can save his head?" asked Max, grinning.

"You mean the *whole* head, *including* the ears?"

"Well, if it's asking too much . . ." Max snickered.

The two of them kept it up like that for a while, a couple of regular comedians. As for me, I just sat there quietly with an expression of mild superiority on my face, as if to say, "Please. I'm afraid this is simply too childish for me to respond to."

Finally Mr. Stringfellow got down to business. First he tested my hair for stiffness by tapping it all over with a spoon. Of course, judging from the way he kept winking at Max, he may also have been trying to tap out a tune. Then he disappeared into his back room for a minute and returned with a dark brown bottle with a cork in it. "Don't know what I'd do without this stuff," he said, holding his thumb on the cork and shaking the bottle vigorously.

"What is it?" I asked uneasily.

"Can't say that I know," he said, pulling out the cork. A wisp of white vapor curled out of the bottle, and a powerful chemical odor flooded the room. I could hardly breathe. "But I use it for everything from softening boots to killing rats."

I only hoped this was another one of his little jokes, because before I knew what was happening, he'd poured whatever it was all over my hair.

Immediately I heard a hissing, bubbling sound, and my eyes went quickly to the big mirror in front of me. My whole head was fizzing and foaming!

I shot a glance at Mr. Stringfellow. His eyes were wide with alarm.

"Quick, Mr. Huff!" he yelled to Max, waving his arms wildly. "It'll eat right through his scalp! Get me a blanket! I'll get the tongs!"

I started out of my chair. *"Scalp?"* I cried. *"Tongs?"*

Only then did I notice that Mr. Stringfellow was chuffing again. He sounded like a steam locomotive on a cross-country race, its throttle wide open. His shoulders shook and his eyes watered, but he never cracked a smile. "Just funnin', Mr. Langsfield, sir," he managed to say. "Everything's under control."

He eased me back into my chair.

I hadn't actually had a heart attack, exactly. Just a severe heart strain. Still, I decided it would be a very long time—maybe even a lifetime—before I ventured into a barbershop again. Even if it meant wearing my hair piled on top of my head in a big bun.

At least things went reasonably smoothly after that. Rolling up his sleeves, Mr. Stringfellow massaged my hair for a while until it collapsed all around the sides of my head into a wet, blobby mess. Then he proceeded to give my hair a "thorough washing." This he did by scrubbing it with a bar of soap until it was good and sudsy and then asking me to step out his side door for a minute, having me bend over, and pouring four or five buckets of water over my head.

Finally, he brought me back inside, sat me back down, and began towel-drying my hair—which, fortunately, seemed to be back to normal.

Max, meanwhile, had found a coin in his suit pocket and was whiling away the time by practicing one of his simpler magic tricks. I figured he was beginning to sort of limber up for Dawn Sharington's party, back in the present.

"Observe!" he said dramatically to Mr. Stringfellow. "Observe that there is nothing, absolutely nothing whatsoever, in my hands." He held up his hands, turning them front and back to show they were empty. Then, with a flourish, he reached out and plucked a coin from under the barber's chin.

Mr. Stringfellow was very impressed, and well

he should be. Max had probably spent a hundred hours practicing palming coins during the past four months, and by now he was so good he made it look easy. After he'd shown you his empty hands, he'd distract your attention with one hand, palm a coin with lightning speed in the other, and then reach out and produce the coin from out of your nose so fast that you'd begin to wonder if you'd put one in there yourself and had forgotten all about it.

"Well, I'll be a ring-tailed lizard!" said Mr. Stringfellow. "Let's see you do that again." He came around and stood in front of Max, leaning forward slightly, his eyes narrowed, ready to watch carefully this time.

"Observe!" Max said again. "Observe that there is nothing—"

He never got any further. Because just then the door swung open and a man stepped inside. At the sight of him, the barber stiffened and his face went white.

It was the same man who had shoved past me earlier on the boardwalk, the one with the shoulder-length blond hair and the pale-blue killer eyes. He looked high-strung, restless, almost hunted. With cat-like movements that were quick and controlled. His gun was slung low on his hip, with the bottom end of his holster tied down around his thigh with a raw-hide string.

But it was his eyes that told me he was a gun-fighter. There was something icy in them, something cold and cunning and dangerous.

Of course, I thought, maybe I'm wrong. Maybe

he's actually a warm and sensitive guy. Maybe he's an insurance salesman or something, and he has this great sense of humor and everyone loves him because he's such a barrel of laughs.

"Be right with you, Mr. Plummer," quavered the barber with forced cheeriness. He coughed nervously. "Won't be a minute. Just let me finish with Mr. Langsfield here." He hurried back over to me and went to work putting some hair tonic on my hair.

Mr. Plummer gave each of us a brief, contemptuous look from his pale, iceberg eyes and then stepped back, leaned against the wall, and began restlessly fingering the hammer of his gun. "Be quick about it," he said, low and hard.

Well, *that* wasn't very funny, but then maybe he just hadn't gotten warmed up yet.

As Mr. Stringfellow was combing my hair, Max and I exchanged a little small talk about the weather, just to lighten things up. But I can't say it was a wild success. Mr. Stringfellow was too scared to say anything, and as for Mr. Plummer, it was obvious that idle chitchat wasn't his cup of tea. He just slouched against the wall, gazing at us with cold disinterest.

The barber finished and I stood up.

As I did, I happened to glance out the window and see a huge tumbleweed rolling by in the dirt street. I'd never seen a real, live tumbleweed before, and this one was bigger than anything I'd ever seen in a western movie. It was enormous! It must have been shoulder high.

"Wow, get a load of that tumbleweed!" I said to Max.

It was the wrong thing to say.

No sooner were the words out of my mouth than the man with the gun shoved violently away from the wall, backhanding a chair out of his way with such force that it flew across the room and smashed against a wall.

In two steps he was in front of me, trembling with rage.

"Who you callin' a tumbleweed?" he said, his voice tight with deadly menace.

# 7

No one moved.

I knew *I* wasn't about to move. I had the feeling it wouldn't be healthy.

"I asked you a question, mister," the gunfighter said to me, his voice hard as steel. "Who you callin' a tumbleweed?"

Before I could speak, the barber piped up to defend me. "Er, excuse me, Mr. Plummer," he ventured in a voice that was high and thin with fear, "but I'm sure Mr. Langsfield didn't mean nothin'. He's a stranger hereabouts, and he—"

The gunfighter silenced him with a look. Then he turned back to me, cold fury in his eyes. "You got three seconds, mister."

Three seconds? Well, I never like to put off until tomorrow what I can do today. Or better yet, in the next three seconds. So I just opened my mouth right up and started talking.

"There seems to have been some sort of misunderstanding here," I began. "I never called you a tumbleweed. I called a *tumbleweed* a tumbleweed. You see, there was this big tumbleweed out in the street, and I—"

*"Yer lyin'!"* he exploded. A vein on his forehead had begun to throb.

I couldn't figure out what was going on. I mean, this guy really did seem to think I'd called him a tumbleweed. But even if I had, what was the big deal? Back where I came from, "tumbleweed" wasn't exactly a fighting word.

One thing was for sure. If this was the way he reacted when he thought I'd called him a tumbleweed, then I'd hate to see what he'd do if I called him a miserable, flap-eared, hog-faced twit with about as much brains as a baked potato.

He'd probably never speak to me again.

All of a sudden, he took a short, quick step backward and stood taut as a stretched wire, his feet apart, his hand hovering near his gun, fingers spread. A twitch had developed at the corner of his mouth. His eyes blazed.

"You called me a tumbleweed," he snarled, twisting off each word as he said it, "and now yer gonna pay fer it!"

I swallowed hard. He was going to draw on me! He was actually going to draw on me! Sure, I was unarmed, but there was something in his wild eyes that told me he wasn't going to let a detail like that stand in his way.

His hand inched closer to his gun. Closer . . .

"Hey," said Max suddenly, "what's this behind your ear?"

Max reached out and plucked a coin from behind the gunfighter's ear. The gunfighter looked startled.

I didn't waste any time.

"Hey, yeah, and what's this in your holster?" I said.

I reached out and grabbed the gun out of his holster.

The gunfighter stared at his gun, then at me, flabbergasted.

"Why, it's a *gun*," I said in a surprised voice. I held it up for all to see. Then I flipped open the cylinder and peered at the chambers. "Well, my word. Look at this. It's all clogged up with these little bullet things." I began removing the bullets one by one. "But don't worry, Mr. Plummer. I'll have it all cleaned out in no time."

The gunfighter's mouth hung open and his eyes were bulging. From the look of him, I was pretty sure he wasn't used to having his gun emptied by a stranger.

Naturally, I was sort of worried that he might just haul off and jump me, but I was hoping he'd noticed that I was about four inches taller and maybe thirty pounds heavier than he was. And just to emphasize the point, I was trying to stand as tall as I could. In fact, I was a little on my tiptoes.

"Say, isn't that the sheriff coming this way?" said Max, pointing out the window.

I guess "sheriff" was the magic word, because the gunfighter instantly came to life. Without even a glance out the window, he moved quickly to the side door, jerked it open, and then turned back to face me. He was still pretty upset. I could tell because his vein was still throbbing and his twitch was still twitch-ing.

I tossed him his empty gun. "Keep that thing cleaned out," I advised him, "and it'll last you a lifetime."

Catching the gun with one hand, he slipped it smoothly into his holster and then seared me with one last murderous look.

"You'll be hearin' from me," he said quietly.

He stepped sideways through the door and dis-appeared.

# 8

Right away I glanced out the front window, but I didn't see any sign of the sheriff—and didn't expect to. I'd already figured Max was bluffing.

"Thanks for the help, partner," I said to Max, grinning with relief. "That was quick thinking with the coin. And mentioning the sheriff wasn't a bad move, either."

"Yeah, well, you did okay yourself," he said, grinning back. "I never knew you were so fast on the draw. Especially with the other guy's gun."

The barber, who had been just standing there looking amazed, suddenly gave a low whistle.

"If you don't mind, Mr. Langsfield, I'd like to shake your hand," he declared, his eyes glowing with admiration. He marched over and shook my hand. For a second there I thought he might salute me, too.

"I never would have believed it," he gushed. "No, sir, I never would have believed it if I hadn't seen it with my own two eyes. You stole his gun right out of his holster! Got the drop on Luke Plummer himself! You've got guts, Mr. Langsfield. Guts and plenty of 'em!"

"Well, sure, yes, *some* guts," I said modestly. I cracked my knuckles. "But you see, Mr. Stringfellow, sometimes you've got to show these gunslingers a thing or two. You've got to show them who's boss, or otherwise they'll get too big for their britches. They'll—"

"You just reached right out and stole his gun clean out of his holster!" Mr. Stringfellow went on, shaking his head in wonder. "Caught him flat-footed and made a ten-gallon fool out of him!" He gave another low whistle. "You must be tired of livin'," he added.

I blinked. "I beg your pardon?"

"I said you must be tired of livin'."

"Well, no . . ." I began uncomfortably. "No, not exactly. I mean, I wouldn't say I was exactly *tired* of living."

"You gotta be," he said firmly. "Anybody who makes a fool of the Tumbleweed Kid has *gotta* be tired of livin'."

I stared at him. "The *Tumbleweed Kid?* What do you mean, the *Tumbleweed Kid?* I thought his name was Luke Plummer."

"Didn't you know?" he asked, surprised. "I thought everybody knew. His nickname's the Tumbleweed Kid. 'Course, nobody calls him that to his face. That'd be suicide."

Now I was *really* confused. "I don't get it," I said. "Why's he called the Tumbleweed Kid? And how come he gets so upset about it?"

"Well, I'll tell you," said Mr. Stringfellow. "It was all on account of what happened down in Tombstone about two years ago."

He paused, remembering, and as he did, his eyes began to twinkle and his shoulders began to shake. Then he let out about eight quick chuffs in a row. Apparently, whatever had happened in Tombstone tickled Mr. Stringfellow's funnybone.

"You see," he went on, "there was Luke Plummer, out in the middle of Allen Street havin' a showdown with a gambler by the name of Nathan King. Plummer was already known as one of the fastest guns in these parts, and King was no slouch, either. Anyways, they were faced off against each other, about thirty feet apart, and were just about to draw, when a big old tumbleweed come rollin' down the street behind Plummer. Accordin' to folks that was there, it was travelin' at upwards of forty mile an hour.

"Well, just as Plummer goes for his gun, he suddenly sees this tumbleweed's shadow rushin' up on him from behind. Naturally, he thinks he's bein' bushwhacked, so quick as greased lightning he spins around, off balance, and gets off two shots into the middle of the tumbleweed before it takes one last bounce, smacks him square in the chest, and knocks him clean over backwards, arms and legs flailin' all over the place."

This image struck Mr. Stringfellow as so enjoyable that it was several seconds before he could go on. " 'Course," he finally managed to say, "that was the end of the gunfight. Nathan King laughed so hard they had to carry him back into the Oriental Saloon and sit him in his chair. As for Plummer, he just sort of got on his horse and rode out of Tombstone, hangin' his head low." Mr. Stringfellow chuffed so hard his eyes watered. "I don't think he visits there often," he added.

"And he's been called the Tumbleweed Kid ever since?" asked Max.

"Sure has," said Mr. Stringfellow, wiping his eyes. "But take it from me, you don't want to call him that when he's around. Fact is, you don't even want to *mention* the word 'tumbleweed' when he's around. Unless, of course, you're . . ."

His voice trailed off as he eyed me meaningfully.

I took a wild guess.

"Tired of livin'?" I asked.

He nodded.

"Tired of livin'," he said.

# 9

As we walked back to the Gulch Hotel, Max and I agreed on several things.

First, as for the Tumbleweed Kid, we agreed that I should stay cool, stay alert, stay out of his way, and, if possible, stay alive.

Second, as for the sheriff, we agreed that I should keep my secret three o'clock appointment with him. I'd told Max about my strange conversation with the sheriff and about how he'd seemed very concerned that "the duck hadn't quacked." Max said there were a lot of perfectly good explanations for why he would say such a thing, but the best explanation, he agreed, was that the sheriff was nutso.

Third, as for my scheduled performance at the Last Chance Theater that night, we agreed that I should not panic and fling myself in front of a passing stagecoach but should somehow get more information. There would be plenty of time for panicking *after* I found out exactly what I was expected to do that night.

And it was right about then that we spotted the handbill. Just outside the hotel, nailed to a post, was a handbill with its ink still wet. DESMOND LANGSFIELD ON STAGE! it announced. THREE NIGHTS ONLY! In small print, it went on to describe the program for each night.

We looked around to be sure nobody was watching, and then I quickly tore the handbill off the post, folded it up, and stuffed it inside my vest.

Fifteen minutes later I was sitting on a cowhide-covered chair in my hotel room, glumly staring at the handbill. Max's room was across the hall, but at the moment he was kneeling in the middle of my room, busily investigating the contents of one of Desmond Langsfield's large leather trunks. It was full of costumes.

"Hey, look at this one!" he said, holding up a three-cornered pirate-type hat and a long maroon jacket trimmed with gold braid.

"Yeah," I sighed. "Nifty."

Once again I ran my eyes over the details of that night's program.

Tuesday Night!
Three Thrilling One-Man Plays!
Conceived and Written by the Actor Himself!
Dramatic, Dazzling, Daring, Delightful!

In Order of Presentation:

1. *Hurricane Jake and the Rattlesnake,* wherein Hurricane Jake awakes one morning to discover a rattlesnake coiled on his chest. Both

his heartfelt fears and his heroic resolves are dramatically rendered.

2. *My Pard, He Cashed in His Chips,* wherein Zachary Pott, a hardworking but unsuccessful prospector for gold, recounts in soul-stirring words the death of his friend and partner of forty years.

3. *A Ghost! A Ghost! I See a Ghost!* wherein Frankie LaRue—a notorious gunslinger, train robber, and cattle rustler—receives a startling visit from a mysterious messenger from the Great Beyond.

No way, I thought gloomily. Obviously, there was no way I could show up at the theater that night. I mean, not in a million years could I fake three whole plays.

Well, I thought to myself, there comes a time in every actor's life when he has to throw back his shoulders, stiffen his upper lip, and skip town. When he has to button up his overcoat, check that the coast is clear, and ride off into the sunset. Never to return. Never to—

"This thing must weigh fifty pounds," said Max.

He was holding up a fancy buckskin jacket with enough fringe and beadwork on it to choke a horse. It was a great costume—rugged but flamboyant—and I found myself sort of regretting that I wouldn't get a chance to wear it. After all, as Desmond Langsfield, I was a pretty impressive-looking guy, and in one of these costumes I'd probably look even more impressive.

I got up and took a look at myself in the mirror that hung over the dresser. Impressive is right, I thought. Wow, what a face! Look at that strong jaw, that wavy black hair, those intense, deep-set blue eyes. And let's not forget my scar. I turned my head slightly, the better to admire the scar on my left cheekbone. It added just the right touch of mystery and intrigue.

No wonder Desmond Langsfield was a famous actor, I told myself. This face had *star* written all over it.

And listen to this great voice, I thought.

"Testing, testing, testing," I said in my deep baritone.

Max looked up. "What? Are we going on the air?" he asked dryly.

I looked down my nose at him, which was pretty easy to do since I was standing up and he wasn't. "Just experimenting," I said loftily.

"Well, let me know if you decide to broadcast," he said. "Of course, you'll have to wait for Marconi to invent the radio first. That'll be in about thirteen years." He chuckled to himself as he went back to work, unlocking a second trunk and beginning to unpack it.

I ambled over, picked up the buckskin jacket, and tried it on. Then I took another look in the mirror. Boy! Wow! I narrowed my eyes. I flexed my muscles. Just call me Hurricane Jake, I thought.

"There are a whole bunch of props in here," said Max, bending over the trunk and unpacking things right and left—a stuffed rattlesnake, a quiver of arrows, a fake sword, a canteen, a map. "And scripts. There're a whole bunch of scripts in here, too. One for each play."

"Scripts?" Here was an interesting development. "Let me see."

Max handed me a stack of scripts and I flipped through them, picking out *Hurricane Jake and the Rattlesnake*.

I leafed through it quickly. Then I checked out *My Pard, He Cashed in His Chips* and *A Ghost! A Ghost! I See a Ghost!* Actually, none of the plays was really very long. And the lines didn't look all that complicated, either.

Hmmm . . .

For a few fleeting moments I could actually picture myself pulling it off. Of course, there wouldn't be time to memorize every line, but maybe I could get the gist of each play, memorize a few key lines, and wing it from there.

I shook myself. No, that was ridiculous, I thought. For one thing, there wasn't time.

I took out my pocket watch. Seven hours till show time. Subtract half an hour for the sheriff and half an hour for dinner, and that left six hours. Six hours . . .

After all, I *was* pretty good at memorizing things. . . . And I *did* look pretty great in this costume. . . .

Besides, I reasoned with growing enthusiasm, if I got into trouble, I could just cut that particular play short and then fill in with a couple of jokes, a few handstands, or maybe even a rousing rendition of the

Camp Wongahana Campfire Song. How could I lose?

Let's face it, I thought nobly, Nellie was counting on me. The whole *town* was counting on me. I couldn't just let them down, could I? And what about Desmond Langsfield? After all, I was occupying his body, wasn't I? So it was up to me to carry the ball for him.

In fact, the more I thought about it, the more it sounded like fun. I'd always sort of wanted to be an actor.

I decided to try a line. I flipped open *A Ghost! A Ghost! I See a Ghost!* and struck a dramatic pose —with my hand hovering above where my gun would be and a look of astonished fear on my face. Then I boomed: *"Stand back, ghost! Or I'll drill you full of holes!"*

Hey, I thought. Was that terrific, or what?

Max was staring at me. He looked impressed.

"Not bad," he admitted. "But I hope you're not thinking what I think you're thinking."

Now, let's see, I thought to myself. How am I going to convince the Worry Wart that the show must go on?

"Max," I began in my best let's-look-at-this-thing-logically tone of voice, "let's look at this thing logically. You have to admit—"

Suddenly, I was interrupted by the sound of running footsteps.

Someone was charging full tilt up the hotel stairs, taking the steps two or three at a time. Reaching the top, whoever it was turned and came thundering down the hall toward our room. Seconds later, there was a frantic hammering on our door that made the walls shake.

Max and I exchanged a questioning look.

"I don't suppose it's room service?" I asked him.

"I doubt it," he said.

I opened the door.

It was Wilbur. Good old Wilbur J. McNabb from the train. Inventor of Wilbur's Why-Not-Be-Handsome Hair Tonic—the very same hair tonic that had given me my recent case of cast-iron hair.

He looked all out of breath. He was panting hard and his face was flushed. He was holding his bright green jacket by one sleeve, dragging it on the floor behind him. His black bow tie had come untied and was dangling across his checkered vest. He was obviously a man in a hurry.

"Hi, fellows!" he said breathlessly. He glanced nervously back down the hall and then stepped quickly inside the room, closed the door, and backed against it. "Nice room you've got here," he said. He looked around. "Does it have a closet?"

"Huh?" I said. "A what?"

"A closet."

"Well, uh, sure," I said. "Right over there."

Taking five or six rapid giant steps, Wilbur crossed the room to the closet.

"I'll just be in here," he said, going in and closing the door behind him.

# 10

Max and I stared at each other in astonishment.

"Did Wilbur just go into the closet?" I asked.

Max nodded. "Unless my eyes are deceiving me," he said.

Suddenly, we heard the sound of running footsteps—again.

Someone was bounding up the hotel stairs, taking the steps two or three at a time. Reaching the top, whoever it was came charging down the hall toward our room. Seconds later, there came the thundering blows of a fist on our door. The walls shook and the windows rattled.

Max and I exchanged another questioning look. "Maybe *this* is room service," I suggested.

"I still doubt it," said Max.

I opened the door.

It was a cowboy.

A tall, lean, muscular cowboy, about twenty years old, with curly brown hair. A cowboy who looked as if he'd been involved in some sort of major mishap in the not-too-distant past. His cowboy hat was battered and torn. His red shirt, bandanna, jeans, and chaps were caked with dirt. His boots had deep scrape marks on them, and one of his spurs was bent.

He looked pretty upset about something, too.

"Where is he?" he demanded, pushing past me into the room. He looked around fiercely. "Where is that no-account skunk?"

He wheeled around and confronted Max and me.

For the first time I noticed he was carrying something. Dangling from his right hand by a thick leather strap was a strange contraption made of wood and large metal springs.

"Skunk, you say?" I said, trying to look helpful.

"That's right, *skunk!*" said the cowboy, thrusting out his chin. "Wears a green jacket. Has a long nose. You seen him?"

Making sure not to look in the direction of the closet, I tapped my chin thoughtfully. "You know," I said slowly, "that's beginning to sound a bit like that chap we met on the train today." I frowned with deep concentration, as if I were straining my memory cells to the fullest. "Wears his hair parted down the middle? Looks a little like a puppy dog?"

"That's him!" declared the cowboy. "That's the miserable skunk, all right. Jest let me get my hands on him, and I'm gonna wrap this thing around his neck."

He brandished the contraption in his hand meaningfully.

"Uh, that's a very interesting-looking gadget," Max observed politely. "What exactly is it?"

"This?" The cowboy gave a bitter snort. "This is what that smooth-talkin' coyote, Wilbur McNabb, sold me. This is one of them McNabb's Miraculous Jumpin' Shoes."

*"Jumping shoes?"* said Max and I together. We leaned forward for a closer look.

" 'Course, this is only one of 'em," explained the cowboy, holding it out where we could see it. "The other one got away from me durin' the trial run. Don't know where it landed."

Max and I examined the surviving jumping shoe. It turned out to be composed of two sturdy pieces of wood, both cut in the shape of large footprints, with two powerful metal springs sandwiched in between— one at the toe and one at the heel. The springs were about eight inches high. Attached to the top piece of wood were two strong leather straps with buckles.

"Mmm, very interesting," said Max. Max has put together some pretty peculiar contraptions of his own from time to time, so naturally he takes a professional interest in other people's peculiar contraptions. "Mr. McNabb invented these shoes, did he? What sort of jumping are they for?"

The cowboy gave another disgusted snort.

"Well, accordin' to that slick-talkin' McNabb, they're good for any general, all-round, all-purpose jumpin' you might care to do. But they're especially good, he said, for trick ridin'. It was the trick ridin' that got my interest."

"Trick riding?" I said. "You mean like on a horse?"

"That's right. Fancy trick ridin', jest like in one

of them travelin' circuses. I always wanted to be a trick rider, so I could show off for my girlfriend, Amy Lou. McNabb said his jumpin' shoes was jest the thing. He said Amy Lou's eyes would bug right outta her head when she saw me.''

Max was giving the springs an experimental squeeze, but they were so strong they hardly budged. "But I don't think I understand," he said. "How can you use jumping shoes for trick riding?"

"That's exactly what I asked McNabb," said the cowboy. "I told him I never heard of no trick rider usin' jumpin' shoes. But McNabb said with his jumpin' shoes I could jump on my horse from upwards of *thirty feet away*. He said what did I think Amy Lou's face would look like if she saw me do *that?* And then he said how would I like to be ridin' down the street at a full gallop and all of a sudden swing off the side of my horse, land on the ground with my jumpin' shoes, and bounce clean back over the horse—all the while holdin' on to the saddle horn. McNabb said I could jest keep on bouncin' back and forth from one side of the horse to the other, pretty as you please. He said what did I think Amy Lou would do if she saw me do *that?* He said she'd prob'ly up and faint dead away.

"Well," concluded the cowboy, "that sounded good to me, so I bought them jumpin' shoes."

I glanced quickly at his battered hat, his dirt-streaked clothes, and his bent spur. "You say you made a trial run of some kind?" I asked politely.

"You bet I did. Figured I'd start off with the easy stuff—jumpin' on my horse. So I went out in the middle of the street and strapped the jumpin' shoes on under my boots. Then I jest stood there a spell, bouncin' up and down real gentle-like, feelin' the power of them springs. McNabb, he led my horse down the street about a hundred feet and held him facin' the other way. When we was both ready, I begun my run.

"Well, I knowed right away I was in trouble. I only got one bounce forwards, and all the rest was *sideways*. Them shoes is too wobbly, and them springs is too powerful! My fifth bounce was an almighty big one. I went sailin' off to the right like I'd been shot out of a cannon, cleared the boardwalk by five feet, and went flyin' through the door of Ma Peterson's Restaurant and Chop House. I come down on one of Ma Peterson's tables and busted it up pretty bad. A coupla chairs, too. Ma, she's *big*. Soon as she seen what I done, she hefted me up by the scruff of my neck and heaved me back out in the street without even breathin' hard."

The cowboy shook his head with disgust.

"I was pickin' myself up outta the dirt when I seen that skunk, McNabb, hightailin' it down the street. So I quick took off this here jumpin' shoe— the other one come off somewhere in Ma's place— and I lit out after him. And here I am." He looked around the room again. " 'Course, I can see he ain't here."

"What made you think he would be?" I asked innocently.

"The feller at the desk downstairs said McNabb asked him which room Mr. Langsfield was stayin' in.

He told him Room 9. This is Room 9, ain't it? Are you Langsfield?"

"Why, yes, I *am* Langsfield. And, yes, this *is* Room 9," I said, trying to look very puzzled. "But you know, I think I may have a possible explanation. There's a little window back down the hall at the top of the stairs. It leads out back somewhere. You don't suppose Mr. McNabb changed his mind and went out that way, do you?"

"That'd be jest like that sneakin', underhanded coyote!" exploded the cowboy. He tipped his battered hat politely but hurriedly. "You gents'll have to excuse me. I got me a varmint to catch. I'm fixin' to learn him a lesson about sellin' folks equipment that ain't up to snuff. Them jumpin' shoes is too wobbly!"

Without waiting for a reply, he bolted out the door and raced down the hall. Seconds later, we heard him climbing out the window, muttering to himself.

After that, all was quiet.

Several seconds passed.

Then, slowly, the closet door opened about a foot and Wilbur's head appeared around the edge of the door.

His eyes darted around the room as he checked to see that the coast was clear, and then he opened the door and stepped out with the dignity of a king stepping out of his royal coach. He had his green jacket draped neatly across one arm.

"Wilbur—" I began sternly.

"Those shoes are *not* wobbly!" he declared huffily. "That young man simply does not know how to jump!"

"Wilbur—"

"In my opinion, this is what comes from spending too much time in the saddle and not enough time jumping!"

"Wilbur—"

"After all," he went on passionately, "there is a *right* way to use a pair of McNabb's Miraculous Jumping Shoes, and there is a *wrong* way. You can't *fight* them. You have to go *with* them."

"Wilbur," I said, "he *did* go with them—right into a restaurant, where he broke a table and two chairs."

Wilbur was not impressed.

"Hmmph," he said, flicking a speck of dust off his sleeve. "In my considered opinion, that cowboy couldn't jump across a *mud puddle* without mishap."

I wasn't at all sure I agreed. I had a feeling the cowboy *could* jump over a mud puddle—just as long as he wasn't wearing a pair of McNabb's Miraculous Jumping Shoes at the time.

# 11

I moved quickly and quietly along the alley, keeping to the shadows. It was three minutes to three, and I had an appointment to keep.

I stopped for a moment and listened. Nothing. I went on, slinking past the back of the Silver Palace Saloon, past the back of the Pioneer Gunsmith Shop. I slipped stealthily around a pile of crates, glanced quickly back down the alley, and knocked twice on the back door of the sheriff's office.

Immediately the door opened, and there was Sheriff Parker standing in the darkened interior, his face in shadow, his silver star shining in the gloom. He motioned me inside.

As I stepped past him, he leaned out the door and glanced both ways down the alley. Then he pulled the door shut and locked it. "Right on time," he said in a low, even voice. "I like a man that's on time."

He jerked his head toward the front, and I followed him past a row of empty jail cells and through another doorway into his main office.

The sheriff had made sure we wouldn't be disturbed. The front door was closed and the window shades had been pulled down. The only light in the room was the little that seeped in from around the dark green shades.

Of course, I still didn't have a clue as to why I was here. Why would Sheriff Parker want a secret meeting with an *actor*? Especially an actor he'd never even met until today. After all, as far as I could tell, this was the first time Desmond Langsfield had ever been to Silver Gulch. So what possible business could he have with the sheriff?

"Coffee?" asked Sheriff Parker, still speaking in a low voice. He was standing over near a wood stove with a blackened coffeepot in his hand.

"No, thanks," I said, following his lead and keeping my voice low, too.

As he poured himself a cup, I took a quick look around the office. The furnishings were pretty basic: a swivel chair in front of a rolltop desk, a small bookcase, a table with several large volumes that looked like law books stacked on it, a straight-backed chair, and, in the corner, the wood stove. On the wall were five or six wanted posters, as well as a gun rack with four rifles on it.

No ducks, I was glad to see. No ducks of any kind. No pet duck, no pictures of ducks, not even a rubber duck on his desk.

The sheriff sat down in his swivel chair, tugged at a corner of his thick black mustache, and looked at me hard. "Pull up a chair," he said.

I moved the straight-backed chair closer and sat down.

The sheriff took a slow sip of coffee, looking at me hard over the rim of the tin cup. Then he put the cup down and looked at me hard some more. Naturally, I assumed we were about to get into some serious duck-talk. But no. Suddenly the sheriff swiveled around, picked up a large piece of tattered yellow paper from his desk, and swiveled back.

"Here's the only one you haven't seen," he said, handing the paper to me.

It was a poem, handwritten in big scrawly black letters.

I rode down the canyon
I rode up the wash
I ambushed the stage
And robbed it, by gosh!

And ifn they ask
How come I done it,
Tell 'em I done it
Jest fer the fun of it!
                    Gentleman John Hooten
                The Rhyming Robber of the Rockies

Up in the right-hand corner someone, probably the sheriff, had written a note in smaller, neater handwriting: "Stuck by bowie knife to the Silver Gulch-to-Harrisville stage, robbed at Twin Peaks Pass at 11:30 A.M. on June 23, 1882." That was a week ago.

I looked up. Sheriff Parker was still studying me, his eyes narrowed.

"What do you make of it?" he asked.

67

I stared at him. My mind was a blank. I'm not good at pop quizzes.

"Let me read it again," I said solemnly.

The sheriff nodded, and I read it again. How did *I* know what to make of it? I mean, *he* was the sheriff, wasn't he? I was just your ordinary, everyday famous actor.

I looked up again. The sheriff was waiting. I had to say *something*.

"The spelling," I said in a low, hard voice, "leaves room for improvement."

The sheriff let out a single bark of laughter. "I see you're a man who likes to play his cards close to his chest," he said, nodding approvingly. "Good. A loose tongue can lead to trouble.

"But there's something more you need to know," he went on. "There'll be a shipment of silver bars leaving town on the morning stage the day after tomorrow. I reckon you know what that means."

"Uh, let's see . . ." I said, racking my brain. "Hooten?"

"Hooten. He'll make a try for it, sure. And it's up to you to make certain he's disappointed."

Up to *me?* What was he talking about? How could it be up to me to stop an outlaw?

"Here's a picture of him," said the sheriff.

He handed me a slightly blurry photograph of a stocky man with a fierce, squinty-eyed expression on his face. He had both guns drawn and was pointing them at the camera like he meant business. His clothes were scruffy and worn and he looked a lot like I'd expect a notorious desperado to look, except for one thing: the long cape with the fur collar that he had draped from his shoulders. I guessed that was his poetic touch.

"How'd you get this?" I asked.

"Hooten had it taken by a traveling photographer and then sent it to me himself, with his autograph on the back." The sheriff gave a wry smile. "Fact is, he sent one to pretty near every sheriff and newspaper in the territory. That's how Hooten is. Loves publicity. Thinks there ought to be a whole flock of those eastern dudes out here writing dime novels about him, like they do about Billy the Kid and the James brothers."

I started to hand the picture back, but the sheriff said, "Keep it. You'll need it."

"Er, thanks," I said reluctantly. I put it in my pocket.

"Sorry I can't give you a likeness of that partner of his, or even a good description. He always wears a flour sack over his head, with holes for his eyes." Sheriff Parker paused and then leaned back in his swivel chair and added seriously, "Don't underestimate those two, Langsfield. They've robbed fourteen stages and three banks, and nobody's laid a hand on them yet."

Great. Terrific. And what was I supposed to do? Track 'em down and bring 'em back alive all by my lonesome? Sure. Why not? And maybe I'd tie one of my hands behind my back and wear a pair of McNabb's Miraculous Jumping Shoes just to make it more challenging.

The sheriff stood up.

"That's it," he said. "You've got a job to do, and I reckon you'll do it. Gentleman John Hooten has to be put out of action before that silver shipment goes out on Thursday."

Obviously the meeting was over. I stood up, too.

"You'll be wanting to keep that," he said, nodding toward the poem in my hand.

I would? Why?

I folded it up and put it in my pocket, along with the picture.

"As for *this*," said the sheriff, picking up a gray folder from his desk and tapping it twice with his finger, "I'll be keeping it in a safe place."

On the front of the folder, in neat letters, was my name—Desmond Langsfield!

"After all," he said with a faint smile, "we wouldn't want it to fall into the wrong hands, would we?"

What did he mean by that? What was in that folder anyway? *Why* wouldn't we want it to fall into the wrong hands?

He plopped the folder back on his desk.

I made a quick decision. It was time to act. I had to get a look inside that folder—and *now*.

It was like our school librarian, Ms. Eliot, always says: "Every question's got an answer; you just have to make sure you're looking in the right place."

That folder was the right place.

I stiffened suddenly and looked up at the ceiling, pretending I'd heard something. "What was that?" I said tensely.

The sheriff looked up. "What was what?"

"On the roof. I thought I heard somebody on the roof."

The sheriff sprang into action. "Stay here out of sight," he said. "I'll handle this."

In two strides he reached the front door. He unlocked it, slipped out quietly, and closed the door after him.

In a flash I was at his desk. I flipped open the folder. There was a letter on top. I read it.

June 16, 1882

Dear Sheriff Parker:

We at Southwest Stagecoach have had quite enough of this fellow Hooten. He obviously believes he can rob our stagecoaches at will, and we intend to show the scoundrel that he is mistaken.

Consequently, we have contacted Pinkerton's National Detective Agency, and they have agreed to assign one of their top agents to the case—a certain Mr. Desmond Langsfield of San Francisco, California. He is, as you undoubtedly know, an actor of considerable renown, and this gives him an ideal cover from which to operate.

Pinkerton's National Detective Agency assures us that Mr. Langsfield is quick-witted, clearheaded, and absolutely fearless. Moreover, he possesses a keen understanding of the criminal mind.

We at Southwest Stagecoach believe that with Langsfield assigned to the case, Hoo-

ten's days are numbered. Please give Langsfield any assistance he may require.

Sincerely,

J. P. Crawford
Southwest Stagecoach Lines

Wow! I thought. An undercover detective! Wait'll
Max hears about this.

Suddenly, I heard footsteps on the boardwalk
outside. I slapped the folder shut and quickly stepped
away from the desk.

The sheriff slipped back inside.

"No sign of anyone," he said.

"Sorry," I said. "I reckon I was mistaken."

"No harm done. Better safe than sorry." He
started for the back door. "You'd better leave the
way you came."

I followed him through the room with the jail
cells. Quietly he unlocked the back door and motioned me through. I stepped out and started down
the alley.

I'd only gone a few steps when the sheriff suddenly called after me in a low voice.

"Langsfield!"

I stopped and looked back.

"Get that duck before it quacks again!"

So it *was* a code. And the duck was Gentleman
John Hooten.

I gave the sort of grim, determined smile that I
thought an undercover Pinkerton detective might give.

"That duck's goose is cooked," I said.

"Good," said the sheriff, and he closed the door
and locked it from the inside.

# 12

Back at the hotel I filled Max in on everything I'd learned.

"So that about covers it," I said when I'd finished. "Basically, Max, it boils down to this: I am a quick-witted, clearheaded, absolutely fearless undercover detective."

Slowly and loudly I cracked my knuckles.

"One of the Pinkerton Detective Agency's top agents," I added. "Also, you may have noticed that I am quite tall and incredibly handsome and that I have a very faint but very mysterious and fascinating scar on my left cheekbone."

Max rolled his eyes. "Oh, sure," he said. "Right. Absolutely."

"It is when I am on a dangerous assignment, Max," I went on dramatically, "that all of my many talents come into play. Then I am cunning and resourceful. I am swift, I am silent, I am quick. I move like the panther." I paused and allowed a faraway look to creep into my eyes. "I am the wind," I added.

Max sighed loudly.

"Naturally," he said. "Of course. I get the picture. But if you have a moment, Windy, do you think you could answer a few small questions for me?"

"Be glad to," I said cheerfully. "Fire away."

"Right," he said. He paced back and forth for a minute, rolling up his sleeves, collecting his thoughts. Then he stopped abruptly in front of me. "Okay, let me get this straight," he said. "First, is it true that Sheriff Parker, Southwest Stagecoach Lines, and Pinkerton's National Detective Agency are all expecting you to capture Gentleman John Hooten before that silver shipment goes out the day after tomorrow?"

He raised his eyebrows as he waited for an answer.

"Well, yes," I admitted. "I guess you could say that."

"And is it true that Hooten is very well armed and possibly extremely dangerous?" He held up the picture the sheriff had given me of Hooten aiming his guns at the camera.

"Well, yes," I admitted again. "Now that you mention it, I suppose so."

Max nodded. "And is it true that you have never personally captured anything larger or more dangerous than our Camp Wongahana Cabin Number 7 mascot? Namely, Fred the Turtle?"

I hesitated. "Well, yes. I mean, I guess so. . . ."

Max folded his arms across his chest and looked very satisfied with himself. "So?" he concluded. "So what exactly do you plan to do?"

He thought he had me, but I was ready for that one. "A very good question," I said crisply, "and I know you're going to come up with a very good answer."

"*Me?*"

"Yes, you." I looked him squarely in the eye. "I know you, Max, and I know I can count on you to put that motor-mind of yours to work and come up with a brilliant plan. One that will make the Pinkerton Detective Agency proud. You're good at that sort of thing."

"But—"

"Besides, I'm going to be a little busy for a while. Don't forget, I'm not only a fearless undercover detective, but I'm also a fantastically famous actor, and I need to practice for my performance tonight. So if you don't mind, I can use all the quiet I can get."

Max objected for a while longer, of course, but I could tell it was just on general principles. Actually, he's never happier than when he's got the old motor-mind in gear, tackling a problem or piecing together a puzzle. Before long he was gazing thoughtfully at the poem the sheriff had given me and was wondering aloud why the sheriff had thought it was so important. A few minutes later he was down on the floor, going through Desmond Langsfield's trunks again, this time looking for clues.

Meanwhile, I got out the scripts for *Hurricane Jake and the Rattlesnake; My Pard, He Cashed in His Chips;* and *A Ghost! A Ghost! I See a Ghost!* and settled down for some heavy-duty rehearsing.

Two hours later I'd made a lot of headway. I'd

read each of the three plays twice, tried on the costumes that went with each play, and paced around the room trying out various dramatic poses to fit the various scenes.

There's no business like show business, I thought to myself in high spirits as I stretched out on the floor in my Hurricane Jake outfit and coiled the stuffed rattlesnake on my chest. I closed my eyes and began snoring loudly. After a minute I pretended to awake with a start. Staring at the rattlesnake eyeball to eyeball, I experimented with several expressions of terrified alarm, took a deep breath, and prepared to deliver my opening line.

Suddenly I heard a weird wheezing sound.

I looked around and there was Max watching me, a mile-wide grin on his face. He was leaning helplessly against the wall, his shoulders shaking, quietly laughing himself silly.

"That snore!" he managed to wheeze. "That expression!"

I eyed him frostily. This was not the sort of behavior a serious actor likes to see in his audience.

"Tonight," he gasped, "I want a . . . I want a . . ." He was having trouble speaking. "I want a . . ."

"Yes?" I inquired.

"I want a front-row seat!" he burst out, and cracked up completely.

When Max cracks up, he goes all out. First he slid down the wall, clutching his stomach and giggling, and then he rolled over behind a trunk, cackling crazily.

Carefully I removed the stuffed rattlesnake from my chest, placed it on the floor, and sat up.

"By all means, Max," I said with great sincerity. "You *should* have a front-row seat. I *want* you to have a front-row seat. After all, maybe you can pick up a few pointers from my performance. Maybe you can learn something about stage presentation and show-biz pizzazz. Something that might help you put some sparkle and style into that magic show you're going to do at Dawn Sharington's house as soon as we get back to the present. I mean, I know you'd like to impress Dawn so much she'll swoon right into your arms."

Suddenly things got very quiet behind the trunk.

"Yes, Max," I went on, warming to my topic, "if you want your ladylove to gaze up at you with those big blue eyes of hers and say breathlessly, 'Oh, Max! Oh, Max, oh, Max, oh, Max!'—then, yes, definitely, I think you should have a front-row seat."

Max's head came up over the top of the trunk. He was blushing like crazy, but he was glaring at me dangerously, too.

I breezed on. "I can see it now. Dawn will snuggle up to you and whisper, 'Oh, Maxie! If you do just one more of those wonderful magic tricks, I won't be able to help myself. I'll just *have* to cover you with kisses!' And then she'll—"

Max came diving over the top of the trunk. He tried a flying tackle, but fortunately I took evasive action and he missed.

Nevertheless, I was forced to postpone my rehearsing for a few minutes while I ran for my life instead.

# 13

The Last Chance Theater was filling up fast.

Max and I were backstage, so we couldn't see what was happening out front—but we could hear plenty. And what we heard sounded a bit like a mad scramble for the last remaining chairs on earth. We heard the sound of dozens of boots pounding across the wood plank floor; the harsh scraping of chairs being dragged around and fought over; wild laughter and loud voices; yelling, yee-hawing, and yipping. Somewhere in the midst of all the racket, a piano player was banging out a lively tune in double time. At the same time, someone with good lungs was doing an imitation of a coyote howling at the moon. And from the back of the theater came Nellie Bradshaw's voice, bellowing above the uproar: "Hank Rafferty! How many times I gotta tell you? Them spittoons is there fer a reason!"

It was fifteen minutes till nine. I swallowed hard. Fifteen minutes till show time.

Nervously I straightened my black, flat-brimmed hat and adjusted my gun belt.

Since I'd decided to do *A Ghost! A Ghost! I See a Ghost!* as my first play, I was wearing my Frankie LaRue gunfighter costume. I looked tough. Extremely tough. Especially with my black gloves and my fake black mustache. Not to mention my black boots, black pants, black gun belt, black shirt, black bandanna, and black hat. In fact, the only things that weren't black were my silver hatband, my silver spurs, and my pair of pearl-handled Colt .45s.

I looked tough, all right, but unfortunately I was feeling about as tough as a teddy bear. All that racket coming from the other side of the curtain had me a little worried, to say the least. All in all, I'd have preferred to hear just the quiet shuffling of feet and maybe a polite comment or two, like "Oh, my! I just *know* this is going to be delightful!"

"Hey, Steve," called Max from over near the edge of the curtain. He'd peered out at the crowd, and now he was grinning over his shoulder at me. "Don't you want to take a look at your audience?"

"Well, yeah, sure," I said, trying to sound casual. "Maybe just one little peek."

I strolled over, spurs jingling, and together we peeked around the curtain.

Uh-oh. Panic time.

Through the smoke and dust that filled the huge barnlike room, I saw what looked like three or four hundred miners and cowboys, gamblers and storekeepers, prospectors and army scouts—all engaged in a free-for-all grab for their seats. Some of them were dragging rough-hewn benches across the floor, trying to get closer to the stage; others were climbing over wooden chairs, leaving muddy footprints behind; and everywhere they were using their elbows freely to make headway.

At the foot of the stage was the piano player, wearing a stovepipe hat and hunched over a long black piano, playing for all he was worth. At the back of the theater, where the entire wall was covered with a collection of antlers and horns, there seemed to be some sort of contest going on to see who could steal the other guy's hat and toss it up onto the enormous moose antlers that were mounted high up near the ceiling.

I spotted Nellie at the door, collecting firearms. And through the smoky haze something else caught my eye—a gaudy green jacket and a black-and-white checkered vest. It was Wilbur! He had stationed himself near Nellie, and with a great show of importance was handing out a little slip of paper to each person who squeezed through the door. From the grand sweep of his gestures, you'd have thought he was handing out thousand-dollar bills. What was he up to now?

Along both walls of the theater, for the full length of the room, was a hand-painted scene of a stampeding buffalo herd. And above the painting, along both walls, was a row of box seats. All of the ladies and most of the more dignified-looking men were up in the box seats. Well, not really *that* dignified. One of them, a large gentleman with a walrus mustache, a starched white shirt, and a long rope, had somehow managed to lasso a chair on the ground floor and was pulling it up to his box.

A scuffle broke out in back and Nellie waded in, swatting people with her slouch hat and yelling, "Break it up, boys, or I'll toss you out on yer caboose!"

I let go of the curtain and staggered back, stunned. *This* was the audience I was supposed to have hanging on my every word?

Max grinned and gave me a go-team-fight sort of whack on the shoulder. "You'll knock 'em dead," he said cheerfully. "And if you don't . . . well, then, they'll probably knock *you* dead." He chuckled to himself.

I gave him my best Frankie LaRue gunfighter glare, but he went right on.

"But don't worry, Steve," he said. "Whatever happens, I'll make sure the world doesn't forget you. After all, as Ed Huff the newspaperman, it's my job to make a full report on your performance. I can see the headline now: 'Desmond Langsfield Bombs in Silver Gulch! Outraged Audience Seizes Actor and Wallops Stuffing Out of Him.' " Max paused and then added, "Of course, I'll jazz it up a bit, make it a little more colorful, you know."

"Speaking of walloping . . ." I said, starting for him.

Just then Nellie pushed the curtain aside and came striding backstage. Right on her heels marched Wilbur, looking important and carrying a big box tied with red ribbon. He nodded a cheery hello to Max and me.

"Jest a coupla more minutes and yer on, Mr. Langsfield," Nellie announced as she disappeared into the wings. A few seconds later she reappeared, carrying a table over her head. She set it down with a bang near the front of the stage, off to one side. "Jest plop yer box down right here, Mr. McNabb. That way folks kin see it durin' the performance. That is, of course, ifn it's all right with you, Mr. Langsfield."

"Uh, sure," I said as Wilbur set the box down on the table. He carefully centered it and fluffed up the ribbon. "What is it?" I asked.

"This here's the door prize," said Nellie, giving the box a thump. "Seemed like a durned fool idea to me at first, but Mr. McNabb here—yer friend and colleague—talked me into it. Said it'd make yer show even more excitin'."

My friend and *colleague?* Just what had Wilbur been telling her? I looked at him sternly. He shifted his weight uneasily and gave me a weak, toothy grin. Then he fluffed the ribbon some more.

"Yep," Nellie went on. "Fer a fee of jest twenty dollars, Mr. McNabb is providin' this here mystery prize. He gave out a slip of paper with a number on it to ever'body in the theater, and soon as the show's over, we're gonna have a drawin'. Meantime, McNabb won't even tell *me* what's in this here box. Ain't that right, McNabb?"

"Er, that is correct," said Wilbur, smoothing down his hair with both hands. "That is absolutely correct. After all, a mystery prize isn't a mystery prize unless it's a mystery. Why," he declared, warming up, "I wouldn't tell my own dear *mother*—God rest her soul—what's in that box! *Wild horses* couldn't drag the secret from me! And may I take this opportunity to add that that is a most impressive costume you're wearing, Mr. Langsfield."

"Don't try to change the subject, Wilbur," I said. "Now, what's—"

"Whoops!" said Nellie, looking at her silver pocket watch. "Less'n a minute till show time. If that curtain don't go up on time, folks is likely to git irritable. And then, a'course, things kin git dangerous."

Less than a minute!

I gulped, and quickly began running over my opening lines in my head: *Wolves! Maybe twenty of 'em. Traveling in a pack—and hungry! I oughta build a fire, but I can't risk it. Not with a posse hot on my trail!*

"I better go stand guard over the firearms," Nellie went on. "Soon as the piano player stops playin', Mr. Huff, you raise the curtain the way I showed you before."

"Right," said Max.

"I'll go with you, Miss Bradshaw," said Wilbur. "Perhaps I can be of assistance in guarding the fire-arms."

"That's right kind of you, Mr. McNabb," said Nellie. She hitched up her jeans, and then the two of them stepped around the curtain and disappeared.

*Wolves! Maybe twenty of 'em. Traveling in a pack—and hungry! I oughta build a fire, but I can't risk it. Not with a posse hot on my trail!*

Max hurried off the stage and into the wings. He grabbed hold of the curtain rope and stood ready to pull.

Quickly I took up my stance in the center of the stage. Earlier Max and I had put out a few props— a saddle and bedroll, a couple of bags of stolen loot, and the wanted poster that Frankie LaRue was going to brag to the ghost about. The painted canvas backdrop showed a night scene with dark hills, a thin crescent of a moon, and the silhouette of a giant saguaro cactus.

*Wolves! Maybe twenty of 'em. Traveling in a pack—and hungry!*

My hands had begun to feel cold and clammy. My knees were weak and my heart was beating like a war drum. Steady, I told myself. Relax. Breathe deeply.

*Wolves! Maybe twenty—*

Suddenly, the piano stopped playing.

I glanced over at Max. He gave me the thumbs-up sign and then began giving the rope a series of long, hard pulls.

The curtain rose.

The audience fell silent.

For several dramatic seconds, I held my pose. Then, taking a deep breath, I threw out my chest and opened my mouth to speak.

SPLAT! I took a big, wet spitball in the exact center of my nose.

# 14

I glanced down fiercely.

It was that little redheaded rat, Junior Sitwell! The very same Junior Sitwell who'd nailed me with his peashooter at the train station earlier that day. I don't know how he'd managed to sneak into the theater, but there he was, hiding under a bench at front row center, lying on his side with his peashooter in hand, silently yukking his head off.

I didn't bat an eye. Lucky for me, we actors are cool under pressure. Quickly but casually I removed the spitball from my nose, said a silent prayer that the bench would collapse on top of Junior, and prepared to go on with the show.

There was only one little problem. *What* show?

With horror, I realized that Junior's spitball had knocked every single solitary thing about the show right out of my head. I'd forgotten my lines; I'd forgotten the character I was playing; I'd even forgotten the name of the play!

*Think,* I thought desperately. *Try to remember. Concentrate.*

I concentrated. But it was no use. My mind was as empty as the Gobi Desert.

Don't panic, I told myself as I gazed out over the room full of expectant faces. Find some way to stall until you can get a look at the script. Yeah, that's it. One glance at that script and it'll all come back to you. Stall. Buy some time. But how?

Suddenly I had an idea.

I flashed a charming smile at the audience. "Ladies and gentlemen!" I began in my deep, smooth baritone. "Before I begin my show tonight, you have a special treat in store for you! We are privileged to have with us here in Silver Gulch a man who is not only a well-known newspaperman, but one of this country's most talented magicians as well. And tonight he has asked me if he can entertain you with one or two of his fabulous tricks."

Out of the corner of my eye I could see Max frantically signaling from the wings. I glanced over quickly and saw him mouthing, "Not me! Not me! Not me!"

"Therefore, ladies and gentlemen," I swept on, "without further ado, will you please welcome . . . the incredible, the amazing, the stupendous . . . *Ed Huff!* Give him a big hand!"

I sprinted off the stage as the audience applauded wildly, whistling and stomping their feet. They seemed to like the idea of a little extra entertainment.

Max, on the other hand, wasn't quite as gung ho. He'd stopped waving his arms and was just standing there gaping out at the stage, his mouth hanging open, his body stiff. He looked sort of like a stuffed fish.

"Just go out there and wow 'em with a trick or two, will you, Max, old buddy?" I said. "I forgot my lines and I need a quick peek at the script." I tried to limber him up a little, moving his arms up and down, rubbing his shoulders, getting his blood circulating again. "It'll be great practice for you, Max. I know you can do it. You're going to be great. Go to it!"

I gave him a gentle push and he began walking out onto the stage, slow and stiff-legged, like a zombie.

"Just remember," I whispered after him. "Lots of pizzazz."

I turned and ran back to the dressing room. The three scripts were on a table. I snatched up the one on top and read the title: *A Ghost! A Ghost! I See a Ghost!* Of course! Just as I knew it would, everything came back to me in a flash. I didn't even have to turn the page. I looked up. *Wolves!* I said to myself. *Maybe twenty of 'em. Traveling in a pack—and hungry!*

I slapped the script down on the table and ran back to the wings, where I was just in time to hear Max nervously saying, "For my first trick, ladies and gentlemen, I will need a volunteer from the audience. Do I have a volunteer, please?"

Immediately two tough-looking men in the front row, sitting a few seats apart, jumped up and said, *"Me!"* They glanced at each other and then scrambled toward the stage, trying to beat each other out.

But they never got there. From behind them, two huge arms reached out and two enormous hairy hands seized them by their shoulders.

"I reckon *I'll* do the volunteerin'," growled a deep voice.

I gave a low whistle. The two men were in the clutches of a huge man—although at first glance I thought he might be a bear. He was massive. He was hulking and muscular. He must have been at least six feet six inches tall and probably tipped the scales at about three hundred pounds. He had long tangled hair that blended in with his bushy black beard, and smoldering black eyes that glowered out from under thick black eyebrows. His buckskin clothes were weathered and worn and looked as if they'd been lived in round-the-clock for the past three years. Around his tremendous shoulders he wore a long, shaggy buffalo robe that hung down to the tops of his fur-trimmed boots.

"I reckon *I'll* do the volunteerin'," he repeated.

The other two guys had gotten a look at him, and they weren't objecting. As soon as he turned them loose, they hightailed it back to their seats.

The big guy climbed onto the stage and started toward Max. The stage shook with every step he took. I had to hand it to Max. He stood his ground. His face was pale and his eyes were like saucers, but he stood his ground.

The big guy took one last step and came to a stop. He looked down at Max and grunted, "The name's Mountain MacLachlan. I'm yer volunteer."

"Er, fine, glad to have you aboard, Mr. Mac-Lachlan," Max managed to say. He had to look almost straight up to talk to him. "And allow me to thank you in advance for your valuable assistance. Now, sir, would you happen to have in your possession a pocket watch?"

Mountain eyed him suspiciously. "Mebbe," he said.

"And would you be so kind as to lend it to me?"

"What fer?"

"Well, uh, you know, for the trick, Mr. MacLachlan." Max took a deep breath and pressed on. "Have no fear, sir, I will return it to you without a scratch."

There was a pause as Mountain mulled that over, glaring down at Max, combing his beard with his fingers. Then, very slowly, he reached under his buffalo robe and drew out a battered old watch on a short chain. Reluctantly he handed it over to Max.

"That there's my grandfather's watch," he said meaningfully.

"And a very fine watch it is, too," said Max, holding it out so the audience could see it. With his other hand he whipped out a white handkerchief from his shirt pocket. "Now, Mr. MacLachlan," he continued, "you see before you a perfectly ordinary handkerchief. Would you care to examine it?"

Mountain took the handkerchief, looked it over carefully on both sides, and turned to the audience. "It's a hanky," he announced.

"Thank you, Mr. MacLachlan," said Max, taking the handkerchief back. "Now watch closely, ladies and gentlemen, as I perform this ancient and amazing feat of magic!"

Holding the watch in the palm of his outstretched

hand, Max snapped the handkerchief a couple of times in the air with his other hand and then, with a flourish, laid it over the watch.

With his free hand, he proceeded to pick up the watch, with the handkerchief hanging down around it. Then, using both hands, he wrapped the handkerchief around and around the watch. Finally, he knelt and placed it on the floor in front of him.

From where I was standing, I would have sworn the watch was inside the handkerchief. But Max is quick. He fools me every time.

Max rose. He looked solemnly at Mountain. He looked solemnly at the audience.

"I only hope, ladies and gentlemen," he said dramatically, "that my magical powers do not fail me now. Otherwise, I am sorry to say, this fine watch will be reduced to a thousand tiny pieces."

Mountain didn't look at all pleased with this announcement. His thick black eyebrows drew together in a suspicious scowl.

Slowly Max raised his right foot above the handkerchief. He started to yell, *"Hai-ya!"* but he never got it out.

Because just then Mountain reached out, grabbed Max by the back of his collar, and lifted him straight up off the ground. Max's feet dangled about a foot above the floor.

"Ain't nobody gonna stomp on that there watch," Mountain growled threateningly, giving Max a little shake.

"Mountain MacLachlan!" roared Nellie from the back of the theater. "You put Mr. Huff down!"

"Yeah!" someone in the first row called out. "Put that feller down, you big ox!"

"Who you callin' a ox?" demanded Mountain, glowering down into the audience. He tucked Max under his arm and started for the edge of the stage.

*"Fight!"* yelled about ten people at once.

I guess "fight" was the magic word. Because even before Mountain had managed to climb off the stage and grab the offender by the hair, people had started taking sides and three or four other fights had broken out all over the theater.

I went into action. I figured I'd better rescue Max—and quick, before Mountain began using him as a club.

I charged out onto the stage, immediately tripping over the table with Wilbur's mystery door prize on it. The table went over, and the box crashed to the floor. The lid came off. A chicken came out.

The chicken was wearing a little black hat on its head! No, it wasn't a hat. It was Wilbur's bow tie, tied on like it was a hat!

Making a break for it, the chicken fluttered off the stage and started on a zigzag course through the audience.

"Hey, the door prize is loose!" yelled Wilbur from somewhere in the back.

From all over the theater there were cries of *"Get the chicken!"*

Within seconds, everyone who wasn't brawling had started after the chicken. People were crashing into chairs and falling over benches, but the chicken held its own, dodging through the crowd, its head held high.

I looked around for Max and spotted him scrambling to safety under the piano. Mountain had dropped him so he could go for the chicken.

SPLUSH! A big, juicy spitball caught me on the chin. I looked down, and there was Junior, still under the bench, crossing his eyes at me and pulling the corners of his mouth out to about his ears. This seemed like as good a time as any to have a little heart-to-heart talk with him. I leaped off the stage and lunged for him. But he was quick. He slithered away, leaving me holding his shoe.

Just then the chicken ran past my ear and I looked up to see eight or ten men, including Mountain, thundering my way. I dived out of the way and scooted under the piano.

Right next to Max.

He scrunched over to make room for me, and we huddled there together, side by side, looking out. All we could see were a few hundred legs going every which way.

Finally, Max turned to me. "Well, what do you think?" he asked cheerfully. "How's my magic show going so far?"

"Great," I said, grinning. "Keep it up. You've got 'em eating out of the palm of your hand."

# 15

It was early the next morning, during breakfast at Ma Peterson's Restaurant and Chop House, when Max dropped the bombshell.

He wolfed down the last of his flapjacks, carefully wiped his mouth with his napkin, leaned across the table, and said in a low voice, "I think I know where Gentleman John Hooten's hideout is."

"You *what?*" I blurted. I almost choked on my bacon.

"Shhh. Not so loud," he said, looking over his shoulder. "You're an undercover detective, remember?"

"Oh, right," I said. I glanced around, too. Then I lowered my voice and went on excitedly. "Now, what's this about Hooten's hideout?"

"Well, I'm not a hundred percent sure, but I think I may have figured out where it is. You know those poems we found in your trunk last night?"

"Sure," I said.

He was referring to the big discovery we'd made

after we'd gotten back to the hotel the night before. We'd returned a little earlier than we'd planned, on account of how the sheriff had kicked everybody out of the Last Chance Theater. He'd shown up right in the middle of the big brawl, fired three shots into the ceiling, and cleared everybody out in about thirty seconds flat. As for Nellie, she told me she was postponing my performance. I was sort of hoping she'd postpone it for a few years, but she said she reckoned twenty-four hours was enough. She said she'd let everyone back into the theater the next night just so long as all them galoots thought it over and decided to mind their manners.

Shortly after we'd arrived back at the hotel, I'd found the poems. I was hanging up some of Desmond Langsfield's costumes when I noticed some papers stuffed in the inside pocket of his Abraham Lincoln coat. I took the papers out and unfolded them.

Poems. Fifteen of them. All on big, greasy, yellow pieces of paper. All scrawled in big black letters. And all the work of one man: Gentleman John Hooten, the Rhyming Robber of the Rockies.

Right away Max and I had concluded several things. First, the poems must have been left by Hooten at the scenes of his various stagecoach and bank robberies. Second, Sheriff Parker must have sent the poems to Langsfield. And third, Langsfield must have thought they were pretty important, because he'd scribbled all sorts of notes all over them. Strange, cryptic notes that Max and I couldn't make sense of. Notes like "Which fork?", "Cross-check with May 13 robbery," and "Rattlesnake or Lone Pine?"

After puzzling over the notes for a while, Max and I had decided to bunk down for the night and tackle the problem again in the morning.

And now, as Max reached for another one of Ma Peterson's buttermilk biscuits, he was looking pretty proud of himself. Old Motor-Mind's mind had obviously been busy.

"You figured out something about the poems?" I guessed.

Max nodded. "I woke up about five this morning, and since I knew you'd throw something large and heavy at me if I tried to wake you up that early, I got out the poems and started studying them again—and Desmond Langsfield's notes, too. And all of a sudden it hit me. I saw what Langsfield was trying to do."

I was impressed. "You did?"

"Yeah. Langsfield had discovered that Gentleman John Hooten, without realizing it, was giving away bits and pieces of information about the location of his hideout in his poems. Here, I'll show you."

He slipped his hand into his coat pocket and pulled out some of Hooten's poems. We moved our dishes aside and he spread one of the poems out on the red-and-white checkered tablecloth. "Get a load of this," he said.

I come outta nowheres
Ridin' high!
I robbed the stage
That ain't no lie!

Now I'm headin' fer home
Ridin' high!
The sun at my back
The dust in my eye!

Gentleman John Hooten
The Rhyming Robber of the Rockies

"Now," said Max, lowering his voice almost to a whisper, "notice how Langsfield underlined the words 'the sun at my back.' And notice how he circled the time and location of the robbery that Sheriff Parker had written up in the corner: '6:00 P.M., Apache Ridge.' And look over here, where Langsfield jotted a note to himself: 'East of ridge.' "

"Yeah, but I don't get it," I said. "What did he mean by 'East of ridge'?"

"Well, I think Langsfield reasoned it this way. At 6:00 P.M. the sun is setting in the west. So if Hooten was riding back to his hideout with the sun at his *back,* then he had to be traveling east. Therefore, his hideout must be somewhere east of Apache Ridge."

"I see what you mean," I said slowly. "But how does Langsfield know that Hooten really had the sun at his back? I mean, maybe Hooten was making it all up, just to make a good poem."

"Sure, that's possible," agreed Max. "But Langsfield was obviously gambling that the truth just crept into the poems without Hooten realizing it. And the more I look at these poems, the more I think Langsfield's hunch is correct."

"Okay, let's say you're right," I said. "Still, east

of someplace called Apache Ridge would cover a lot of territory, wouldn't it?"

"Sure, but there are other clues, too. Look." He laid another poem on top of the first one and leaned over it eagerly. "Like in this one. Langsfield underlined 'cross the dry riverbed,' and then he scribbled, 'Spirit, Rio Blanco, or Little Chuckwalla' over here. I figure those must be the names of rivers that are normally dry."

"I get it," I said, beginning to catch his excitement. "So then he'd look to see which of these rivers is east of Apache Ridge, right? And with enough other clues, he'd be able to pinpoint where Hooten's hideout must be."

"You've got it," said Max.

"But what I don't understand," I said, "is how Langsfield knew where all these places like Apache Ridge are. I mean, he's from San Francisco, not from around here."

"That's exactly what I wondered myself," said Max. "But then I remembered seeing *this*." He reached into another pocket and withdrew a large folded-up piece of paper. He unfolded it and spread it out on the table.

It was a map.

"I sneaked into your room while you were sleeping this morning and dug this out of one of Langsfield's trunks. It was in with the stage props. I remembered seeing it yesterday, but at the time I'd assumed it was just one of the props."

He tapped the center of the map. "Look, here's Silver Gulch. And see over here? Apache Ridge. I've checked all the other places mentioned in Langsfield's notes, and they're all on the map. *And,*" he said, glancing around quickly to be sure no one was paying any attention to us, "feast your eyes on *these.*"

He pointed to two small red dots, a couple of inches apart, that someone had inked in near the southeast corner of the map. One was near Loco Springs and one was in Rattlesnake Canyon.

"I'm positive that Desmond Langsfield put those dots there," said Max. "I checked, and they mark the two locations that fit all the clues he had so far."

"Wow," I burst out. "You mean we've actually got it narrowed down to two possibilities?"

"One," said Max, grinning.

*"One?"*

"Yes, one. Remember the poem Sheriff Parker gave you yesterday afternoon in his office? It was from the robbery at Twin Peaks Pass last week. Desmond Langsfield never had a chance to see that particular poem. But you and I have."

Max leafed through the poems and produced it. "Look at the first stanza."

> I rode down the canyon
> I rode up the wash
> I ambushed the stage
> And robbed it, by gosh!

"Now, look at the map," Max went on. "Both of these red dots are pretty close to Twin Peaks Pass. But if Hooten rode down a canyon and rode up a wash on his way to the pass, then the starting point that makes the most sense is *this* one." He tapped one of the dots triumphantly with his finger. "In Rattlesnake Canyon."

So! Rattlesnake Canyon! I turned the map around so I could see it better. "You're brilliant, Max," I said with real admiration.

Using the scale on the map, I quickly estimated the distance from Silver Gulch to Rattlesnake Canyon. It was only ten, maybe twelve miles at the most.

I stood up.

"Let's rent us some horses and hit the trail," I said.

Max choked on his milk. "Huh?"

"Here's the plan. First we pay Ma Peterson for this fine breakfast. Then we go down to the livery stable at the end of town; we rent a couple of horses; we ride out to Rattlesnake Canyon; and we find Hooten's hideout."

"Oh, well, naturally," said Max. "And then we go in shooting. Except that since we don't have any guns, we go in yelling. We yell, 'Get your hands up, Hooten, or we're gonna throw ourselves into your line of fire and you'll have to use two perfectly good bullets on us!' "

"Who said anything about *capturing* Hooten?" I scoffed. "We're not going to capture anyone. We're just going to see if your theory is right, that's all. Don't you want to know whether Hooten's hideout really is in Rattlesnake Canyon?" I tried to sound reasonable and responsible. "We don't have to get close. We can check things out from a distance. A large distance."

"How large a distance?" Max asked doubtfully.

Ha! The Worry Wart was weakening. I had him now.

"A *very* large distance. A quarter mile. A half mile." I decided to appeal to his nobler instincts. "After all, Max, we can't very well turn this information over to Sheriff Parker unless we know it's right, can we? What if it's wrong? What if Hooten's hideout isn't anywhere near Rattlesnake Canyon? Desmond Langsfield's reputation as an undercover detective would be shot."

"Shot," muttered Max. "That's exactly what I'm worried about." He gave a deep sigh and stood up. "Okay, you win. Just give me time to find a lawyer and make out my will first."

# 16

It was high noon and hot as Max and I reined our horses to a stop at the top of a rise and surveyed the rugged country around us.

I reached forward and patted my horse's neck while Max consulted the map. Silver Gulch was an hour's ride behind us. Sweeping away to the south and west was open country, dry and dusty and dotted with high, red-rock buttes. To the east, ahead of us, were tall mesas, broad and flat on top and cut by deep canyons. And beyond the mesas was the high country, soaring into jagged, rocky peaks.

The West! I thought to myself, inhaling deeply. The Wild West! And just think, I'm an undercover Pinkerton detective! Riding out in search of a dangerous outlaw. Risking my life to bring law and order to a lawless land!

I squared my shoulders and sat a little taller in the saddle. Yes, I thought, narrowing my eyes keenly, I think I could learn to like being an undercover detective. Bringing 'em back alive might be sort of nice. Better than nice. It could be sort of terrific.

"We're right on course," announced Max, stuffing the map back into his saddlebag. "We head straight for that mesa." He shielded his eyes from the sun and pointed east. "There's a spring at the base of it, next to a big jumble of boulders. From the spring, we just follow the cliffs around to the right, and the second canyon we come to should be Rattlesnake Canyon."

I squinted into the distance. The undercover Pinkerton detective rides again, I thought to myself. And he always gets his man.

I pulled my hat down low over my eyes. Max was watching me, so I took a swig of water from my canteen and slowly and dramatically wiped my mouth with the back of my hand. I thought I looked pretty good doing it, so I did it again. Then I cracked my knuckles.

"Let's move 'em out," I said.

Someone snorted. Either Max or his horse, I don't know which.

"This way, General Custer," said Max, and we started down the slope, our horses leaning back on their haunches as they slipped on the loose dirt.

We rode across a series of low hills toward the mesa, with the sun beating down on our shoulders. It was desolate, quiet country. For miles around, all we could see was rock and cactus and low brush. The only signs of life were an occasional lizard scurrying for cover, a couple of hawks circling overhead, and a lone coyote loping along a nearby ridge, watching us over his shoulder as he ran. Away to the south, the wind kicked up dust devils that whirled furiously as they moved slowly over the land for several seconds and then disappeared.

As we rode along, Max and I worked out a strategy for spotting Gentleman John Hooten before he spotted us. We knew we couldn't just go riding right into Rattlesnake Canyon. If Hooten really did have his hideout there, we could come on him suddenly, around a bend in the canyon or something. Besides, we knew Hooten had a partner—the guy who wore a flour sack as a mask whenever they robbed stages —and that meant our chances of being seen were even greater. For all we knew, Hooten kept his partner posted as a lookout somewhere in the canyon.

So we decided to take a peek from above.

Max's map showed an old Indian trail leading to the top of the mesa, and we agreed to try to find it. If we could get to the top, we figured we could peer into Rattlesnake Canyon from various points along the rim, without any chance of being seen.

It was an excellent plan, if we did say so ourselves, and by the time we reached the spring at the base of the mesa, Max and I were both in top spirits. I felt great that we had a good chance of finding Hooten's hideout; and Max felt great that we had a good chance of living to tell about it.

The spring fed into a small, clear pool shaded by a rock overhang. It would've made a nice spot to rest, but we couldn't take the time. We had a job to do. So we stayed just long enough to water our horses, splash some water in our faces, and fill our canteens.

Then we swung back into our saddles and reined our horses around.

Suddenly, a shot rang out and a bullet zinged by my ear.

"If one of you fellers moves so much as one tiny muscle," said a gruff voice, "my next shot is gonna empty a saddle."

I froze. I could take a hint. I mean, I certainly didn't want my saddle emptied unless I'd made a formal dismount.

Slowly I edged my eyes a few degrees to the left. Standing on top of a boulder, both six-guns trained on us, was a stocky man with a fierce, determined look on his face. Draped over his scruffy clothes was a long black cape trimmed with fur. The cape fluttered slightly in the breeze.

I recognized him right away from the photograph the sheriff had given me. It was Hooten. Gentleman John Hooten, the Rhyming Robber of the Rockies.

Suddenly, from behind us, there came another voice. Not gruff this time. But cold and quiet and laced with hatred.

"Well, now, ain't this nice," said the voice. "Mr. Langsfield's come a-callin'."

My heart almost stopped. That voice was familiar.

Slowly I turned in my saddle and looked back over my shoulder.

Bad news. The worst. It was Luke Plummer, alias the Tumbleweed Kid.

# 17

An hour later, Max and I had accomplished part of
our mission. We'd found out where Hooten's hideout
was. Of course, we were prisoners in it, but still, I
always try to look on the bright side.

Hooten and the Tumbleweed Kid had escorted
us there at gunpoint—into Rattlesnake Canyon, just
like Max had figured. We must've ridden at least a
mile into the canyon from its mouth, following a dry
streambed most of the time. The canyon was deep
and winding and narrow—so narrow that we often
had to ride single file, the red-rock walls rising ver-
tically on either side of us for several hundred feet,
like skyscrapers. At one point, I could've reached out
and touched both sides of the canyon with my hands.

Finally the canyon opened up, becoming wide
and flat. And almost immediately, over near the left
wall and tucked in behind a rock the size of a barn,
was the shack.

I had to hand it to Hooten. It was a fantastic
place for a hideout.

A fantastic *place* for a hideout, yes, but I can't say much for the hideout itself. I don't know what Gentleman John had done with all his stolen loot, but he sure hadn't put it into interior decorating. The sum total of the furnishings in the one-room shack was a pine table that wobbled when you leaned on it, a single kerosene lamp that hung at a slight angle above the table, two chairs and two empty powder kegs for sitting, a couple of bunks against the wall, a few candles stuck in bottles, and a piece of broken mirror on the wall. Daylight streamed in through cracks in the walls.

"I'll jest put these things right here, in case I need 'em in a hurry," said Hooten, looking hard at Max and then at me as he laid both of his guns on the table in front of him.

Max and I were facing him, sitting side by side on the two chairs, which had been placed a little way back from the table. Behind Hooten, standing off to one side and leaning tensely against the wall, was the Tumbleweed Kid. I don't think he'd taken his pale-blue killer eyes off me once since we'd been captured. His gaze—cold and steady—was the gaze of a snake waiting to strike. A hint of a sneer was on his thin lips. His lean fingers played idly with the hammer of the gun in his low-slung holster.

Gentleman John Hooten shoved up the sleeves of his sun-faded red flannel shirt, planted his elbows on the table, and squinted at Max. "Well, now, Mr. Huff. It was a pure pleasure findin' you there at the spring. You done saved us a trip to town. Me and my pardner, here, was jest on our way into Silver Gulch to kidnap you."

106

To kidnap *Max?* They were after *Max?*

"Yes, sir, Mr. Huff," Hooten went on, enjoying himself. "Yer quite a prize. And we gotcha, don't we?"

I was good and confused. I'd been sure they were after *me*. I'd figured they wanted me for one of two reasons. Either they'd somehow discovered that I was an undercover Pinkerton detective and they wanted to be sure to fill me full of lead, or else the Tumbleweed Kid had told Hooten about how I'd taken his gun away from him in the barbershop and they wanted to be sure to fill me full of lead.

"Er, yes, you've got me, all right," said Max, looking as confused as I was. "But what exactly do you want with me?"

"You done asked me an easy one, Mr. Huff," said Hooten, "and I'm gonna answer you plain and simple. Yer a newspaperman and yer gonna write a story 'bout me that's so ripsnortin' excitin' that it's gonna make me famous from one end of this country to the other."

"But—" protested Max.

"Ain't no buts about it!" declared Hooten, pounding the table with his fist. "Ain't I robbed fourteen stages and three banks? Ain't I writ a poem 'bout ever one of 'em? Confound it! It's high time I was gittin' the credit I deserve!"

Behind him, the Tumbleweed Kid—without ever taking his eyes off me—was slowly rolling himself a cigarette.

"But Mr. Hooten," said Max, "aren't you already famous?"

Hooten gave a snort that could've been heard

107

halfway to Silver Gulch. "I ain't hardly famous at all compared to what I'm fixin' to be!" he burst out. "Sure, folks has heard of me down in Tombstone. And sure, they's heard of me over in Mule Junction. But I'm talkin' 'bout *real* fame. New York City! Chicago! San Francisco!"

He jumped up, jammed his guns back into his holsters, and rushed over to a bunch of books that were piled on the floor next to one of the bunks.

"Wait jest a minute," he said over his shoulder. "I got somethin' I wanna show you." He began rummaging through the pile.

The Tumbleweed Kid had finished rolling his cigarette. He licked the paper lengthwise and sealed it closed. Then he stuck the cigarette into the corner of his mouth, struck a match on the wall behind him, and lit up. The smoke curled up past his icy eyes, which, naturally, were still trained on me.

Just lucky for him, I thought to myself, that our Health Sciences teacher, Ms. Buckworth, wasn't here. She'd march right over, bat that cigarette out of his mouth, and deliver him a lecture on smoking he wouldn't soon forget.

Gentleman John returned with an armload of books and dumped them on the table in front of us.

"Take a look at these here dime novels," he said.

The books were like paperbacks, but larger, more like the size of magazines, and they had dramatic drawings on the front. Drawings of men in fringed buckskins or cavalry uniforms or cowboy outfits, doing things like wrestling with bears or shooting over their shoulders as they galloped along on their horses. The books had titles like *Jesse James, the Badman of the Plains; The Adventures of Wild Bill, the Pistol Prince;* and *Bowie Knife Ben, the Little Hunter of the Nor'west.*

"Jest look at 'em!" said Hooten indignantly. "There ain't no reason under the sun why Jesse James and Sam Bass and Billy the Kid and some of them other fellers oughta be hoggin' all the glory. It ain't fair! Why, them fellers didn't even write no poetry or nothin'! Prob'ly couldn't put two words together and make a rhyme to save their souls!"

The Tumbleweed Kid still hadn't taken his eyes off me. He just stood there, his cigarette between his teeth—staring, staring, staring at me. I wished he'd at least *say* something. Something like, "Anyone for checkers?"

"Well, Mr. Huff?" said Hooten, folding his arms across his chest and looking sternly at Max. "Let's hear yer answer. You gonna write a story 'bout me, or ain't you?"

"Uh . . ." said Max. "Well . . ." He chewed his thumbnail the way he does when he's thinking hard.

I held my breath. Come on, Max, I thought. Play along. You've *got* to play along. You've got to buy us some time, so we can think of a way out of this.

Max stopped chewing on his thumbnail.

"You know, Mr. Hooten," he said, "it might be an interesting project at that. Of course, I'd need a lot more information. You know, about your childhood, your hobbies, your favorite robbery, things like that."

Good old Max.

Hooten's eyes lit up. "Ain't no problem there,"

he said. "I had me a fascinatin' childhood. And hobbies? I got *lots* of hobbies!"

"Well, all right, then," said Max. "But ripsnortin' stories don't just write themselves, you know. You've got to have details. Colorful details, and plenty of them."

"Don't you worry 'bout that, Mr. Huff," said Hooten. "I'm crawlin' with colorful details. Jest take my name, fer instance—the Rhymin' Robber of the Rockies."

"It's colorful, all right," said Max, nodding with approval. "I suppose you grew up in the Rocky Mountains, did you?"

"Never been there in my life," said Hooten proudly. "I made that name up all by myself. Us poets has gotta use our imaginations. Truth is, the only mountains I ever seen with my own eyes is the Rabbit Mountains, jest east of here a ways. But I warn't about to call myself the 'Rhymin' Robber of the Rabbits.' It ain't got no dignity."

"You made the right decision," said Max firmly. "I *like* the 'Rhymin' Robber of the Rockies.' It has a wonderful, rich, meaningful ring to it."

"My own way of thinkin' exactly!" declared Hooten happily. "By golly, Mr. Huff! I knowed you was the right man fer the job!"

Suddenly, with a quick catlike motion, the Tumbleweed Kid pushed away from the wall. Flicking his cigarette out the open window, he strode to Hooten's side.

He jerked his thumb in my direction.

"What about *him?*" he snarled. "We don't need *him,* do we?"

# 18

I wasn't very happy with the Tumbleweed Kid's tone of voice. And I wasn't very happy with the way Gentleman John Hooten just stood there, looking like he couldn't for the life of him think of any reason why they needed me.

I broke into a sweat. If Hooten turned me over to the Tumbleweed Kid, I was going to be in big trouble. Big, big, *big* trouble.

"Of course you need him," piped up Max. "If you want to be famous, you *definitely* need him."

Hooten looked surprised. "Oh?" he said. "How do you reckon?"

I was wondering the same thing myself.

"Well, you may not know this," said Max, very businesslike, "but Mr. Langsfield here has helped to publicize several well-known outlaws—such as Billy the Kid, Frank Reno, and the James brothers."

It was clear from Hooten's expression that he didn't know this. Which wasn't surprising, since Max had just made it up on the spot.

Max went on. "Yes, indeed. He's written one-man plays about each of these daring desperadoes, and then he's performed these plays in countless cities and towns all the way from San Francisco to Chicago. Not only that, but just yesterday he told me that he's currently working on a play about *you,* Mr. Hooten."

*"Me?"* said Hooten. "A play 'bout *me?"* He was all ears.

"Yes, *you,"* said Max emphatically.

I cleared my throat. It was my turn.

"If it's all right with you, Mr. Hooten," I said, "I'm going to call it *Gentleman John Hooten, Daredevil Outlaw of the West."* I paused to let that sink in. Judging from Hooten's face, I was doing pretty well, so I went on. "And the subtitle would be *I Robbed, I Robbed, I Robbed the Stage!* Of course, that's from the poem you attached to the stage you robbed yesterday. I hope you don't mind my using it. I mean, it's *your* poem, so maybe you wouldn't want me to—"

"You kin use it!" said Hooten eagerly.

"Good," I said. "Great. You know, Mr. Hooten, I don't mind telling you that your poem and your robbery were a real inspiration to me, and I just know this is going to be one of my best plays ever. I was up half the night working on it, in fact."

Hooten was looking more or less delighted, but the Tumbleweed Kid wasn't buying it. "Yer lyin' through yer teeth!" he exploded. "You ain't writin' a play 'bout Hooten, and you know it!" The vein on his forehead had begun to throb. "Yer a—"

"You jest hold yer horses, Luke!" Hooten broke in angrily. "There ain't no call fer you to go sayin' a thing like that!" He looked back at me. "You go right ahead, Mr. Langsfield. Tell me some more 'bout this here play."

"Well, let's see," I said. I leaned forward in my chair and fixed Hooten with a steady gaze. "It opens with a night scene," I said in a low, dramatic voice. "The curtain rises, and there you are, standing in the pale moonlight. On the ground is your saddle. Also, your bedroll. Also, two bags of loot from the stagecoach you've robbed only hours before. You're facing to the left, toward the dark trees at the side of the stage. You stand motionless. Your cape is draped dashingly over your shoulders. Your body is tense. You are listening."

I paused. Hooten's eyes were wide. I went on.

"The seconds tick by. The audience doesn't even dare to breathe. Finally, you speak. *'Wolves!'* you cry. *'Maybe twenty of 'em. Traveling in a pack—and hungry! I oughta build a fire, but I can't risk it. Not with a posse hot on my trail!'* "

I relaxed back into my chair. "It goes on sort of like that," I said nonchalantly. "Like it?"

"By thunder, you *bet* I like it!" exclaimed Hooten. "That there's genius, Mr. Langsfield. Pure genius!" He turned to the Tumbleweed Kid. "Ain't that genius, Luke?"

The Tumbleweed Kid grumbled something about genius, his foot, and then he skulked back over to the wall and leaned against it again. For the time being, he was beaten—but he wasn't liking it. He glared at me like a giant lizard that had just had its dinner taken away from it.

But I hardly even noticed. I was feeling pretty

good, all things considered. Max and I had bought ourselves some time. With a little luck, we could use that time to figure a way out of this situation.

"Yes, sir, Mr. Langsfield," Hooten went on, sounding pleased as punch, "I wasn't plannin' on havin' you with us, but now I kin see I was wrong." He looked back and forth between Max and me. "All right, men, here's the plan. First, we'll wait right here till sundown. Then we'll all go into Silver Gulch and capture the whole town and rob ever'body."

Max and I just stared at him. Had he said "rob"? Had he said "we"?

"See, me and Luke is gonna commit the crime of the century tonight, and you two fellers is gonna be right there with us. Side by side, so's you kin see us in action up close. Then you kin write yer story 'bout me, Mr. Huff. And, Mr. Langsfield, maybe you kin pick up a few colorful details fer yer play."

Max and I just kept on staring at him. Neither of us seemed to be in any condition to say anything.

Hooten sat down on a powder keg, leaned forward over the table, and squinted at us. "Now here's the lowdown," he said. "At nine o'clock tonight, jest 'bout ever'body in town is gonna be in the Last Chance Theater, waitin' to see Mr. Langsfield's show. There ain't nobody gonna be armed, 'cause they're all gonna check their hardware at the door. That's jest where they'll be makin' their mistake. The four of us is gonna slip inside, and then me and Luke is gonna capture ever'body in the theater and relieve 'em of all their valuables."

Hooten banged the flat of his hand on the table.

114

"Jest think!" he said excitedly. "We're gonna hold up a *whole town*. You ever heard of Jesse James holdin' up a *whole town?* If this don't make me famous, nothin' will!"

The Tumbleweed Kid strolled over and stood beside Hooten. His cold eyes flickered over to Max and then came back and stayed on me. "Make one false move while we're in town," he said, low and threatening, "and I'll know what to do about it."

I swallowed hard. I believed he did.

"Hey, I jest had an idea!" said Hooten. "Long as yer gonna be with us at the theater, Mr. Langsfield, you kin introduce me—right there on the stage! You and me kin sneak in the back door, see, behind the stage. And then, jest when Luke and Mr. Huff come in the front door, you kin march out on the stage and explain to ever'body that they're 'bout to be robbed by the famous Gentleman John Hooten, the Rhymin' Robber of the Rockies. That'll be my signal to come strollin' on out with my guns drawn."

I gave a quiet groan. Oh, terrific, I thought to myself. I'm sure this is just what the sheriff had in mind when he told me to capture Hooten. Not only had *Hooten* captured *me,* but now I was actually going to introduce him to practically the entire town so he could rob them silly.

"Tell you somethin' else you kin do, Mr. Langsfield," Hooten added, "which would be a powerful big help. While me and Luke is holdin' our guns on the audience, you kin pass the sack 'round and collect ever'body's money and gold dust and jewelry and suchlike."

115

I gave another groan. Great, I thought. Fantastic. Now I'm going to be passing the sack. The sheriff is going to be tickled pink when he hears about *this*.

From now on, I thought glumly, just call me Desmond Langsfield, undercover Pinkerton detective and big-time thief.

# 19

The only sound was the steady drumming of hoofbeats as we rode through the cool night air, four abreast. The full moon was low in the sky, and all around us were the shadowy shapes of rocks and low hills. Ahead of us, the lights of Silver Gulch shimmered in the distance.

By now, I thought, a huge crowd would be gathering outside the Last Chance Theater. In a few minutes, Nellie would throw open the door, and the citizens of Silver Gulch would pile in, elbows flying, and begin revving themselves up for a whale of a show.

Little did they know.

We rode hard, down into a shallow gully and up the other side. The pounding of our horses' hooves was like a constant roll of thunder. To my left rode Hooten. To my right rode Max, and beyond him, the Tumbleweed Kid.

No one spoke.

Unless, of course, you counted the occasional mutterings of Gentleman John Hooten as he rehearsed the poem he'd written for his upcoming crime of the century. He'd finished it late that afternoon and right away tried it out on Max and me. We'd assured him it was a jim-dandy. It went:

> I went and robbed
> The whole town's pockets!
> I took their gold
> I took their lockets!
>
> I ride tall
> And I ride free!
> Try as you kin
> You'll never ketch me!
>> Gentleman John Hooten
>> The Rhyming Robber of the Rockies

Actually, Max and I had hopes of proving him wrong about the "you'll never ketch me" part. Earlier that day, when Hooten and the Tumbleweed Kid had gone outside to feed and rub down the horses, Max and I had put our heads together and quickly come up with a plan.

Or, to be more precise, with Operation Conk.

Operation Conk was to go into effect after we'd arrived in town. Max and the Tumbleweed Kid would be heading for the front of the Last Chance Theater, and Hooten and I would be heading for the back. Luckily, Max and I knew something about that back door that Hooten didn't. Just inside it, against the wall, was a big table where we'd put all the props I was supposed to use in my plays—including the props for *Hurricane Jake and the Rattlesnake*.

*So*. The moment I stepped through the door, I'd grab the stuffed rattlesnake by the tail and flip it at Hooten, maybe giving a little scream just to add to the dramatic effect. Then, while he was juggling the snake in panic, I'd grab Hurricane Jake's big black frying pan and conk Hooten a good one on the noggin. Next, I'd dash out the door, run around to the front of the theater, slip in the front door, sneak up behind the Tumbleweed Kid, and conk him a good one, too.

Providing I didn't get shot in the process, I thought with satisfaction, Operation Conk should wrap things up nicely.

"From here on," said Hooten suddenly, "don't nobody say nothin'. We're goin' in quiet-like."

We'd reached the outskirts of Silver Gulch. Slowing our horses to a walk, we started down the main street.

The whole town seemed quiet and deserted, except for one place: the Last Chance Theater, a couple of blocks ahead on the right. Lights blazed through the open windows, flooding the street outside, and a wild jumble of shouting, laughing, whooping, and hollering shook the air. It was a wonder the walls hadn't fallen down.

Just about everyone in town must have been packed inside, waiting for my performance.

We turned right, down a side street, and then left at the next corner. Quietly we approached the rear of the theater and dismounted. Hooten and the Tumbleweed Kid tied the horses to a rail. Loosely— for a fast getaway.

"Me and Langsfield'll wait two minutes before we go in," Hooten said in a low voice to the Tumbleweed Kid. "That oughta give you and Huff time to git in the front door."

The Tumbleweed Kid gave a short nod. Then he took his gun out of his holster and tucked it inside his coat so he could smuggle it into the theater. As for the flour sack he usually wore as a mask, he and Hooten had agreed back at the hideout that he wouldn't wear it for this little outing. Now that they were going to commit the crime of the century and be famous all across the nation, the Tumbleweed Kid had decided to go public.

Besides, he couldn't very well buy a ticket and slip in the front door unnoticed while wearing a flour sack over his head.

The Tumbleweed Kid signaled Max, and the two of them started down the narrow space between the theater and the blacksmith shop. But after only a couple of steps, the Tumbleweed Kid stopped, turned abruptly, and shot me one last ferocious look. It was a look that said, "Just try and double-cross us, worm, and it'll be the last mistake you ever make."

I raised my eyebrows and shot him back a look of my own. I hoped it said, "Oh, yeah? Well, maybe you'd care to go soak your head, toadface."

The Tumbleweed Kid turned away with a sneer on his twitching lips. Just then, Max managed to flash me the thumbs-up sign, and I saw him mouth the words "Operation Conk." I nodded back.

It was up to me now.

Max and the Tumbleweed Kid disappeared down the dark passageway. Quietly, Hooten and I moved to the back door and waited. Hooten got out his watch, and keeping one eye on me and one on the watch, began muttering under his breath, "I went and robbed the whole town's pockets. . . ."

Trying to ignore him, I ran over Operation Conk rapidly in my mind: Step through the door. Grab the stuffed rattlesnake. Toss it at Hooten. Grab the frying pan. Conk.

It should be easy enough. Grab, toss, grab, conk. Nothing to it.

"*Now,*" said Hooten, nudging me.

This was it.

I took a deep breath and tensed my muscles for action. Then, with Hooten right behind me, I went up the steps, opened the door, stepped through, and grabbed for the rattlesnake.

It was gone!

So was the frying pan! So was the table!

I groaned out loud. Someone had moved the table—but where? I looked around frantically.

"Let's git movin'," said Hooten, pushing past me into the room.

My mind was racing. "Uh, say, Mr. Hooten," I stammered. "There's a table with some really interesting props on it around here somewhere. If you have a few minutes, maybe we could go look for it."

"Quit stallin', Langsfield," he said. "I got me an appointment with destiny."

I groaned again.

So much for Operation Conk.

Maybe, I thought with a sinking feeling, an undercover Pinkerton detective *doesn't* always get his man.

# 20

"Mr. Langsfield! Am I glad to see you! You got here just in time!"

It was Wilbur. He'd been peeking out at the audience when Hooten and I appeared around the backdrop, but he let go of the curtain as soon as he saw us and rushed over to greet me. He pumped my hand and then straightened his checkered vest and smoothed down his hair with both hands.

"Nellie was getting worried," he said, sort of yelling to be heard over the noise of the audience. "It's after nine, and the crowd's getting a bit restless."

Restless was right. It sounded like a full-scale riot was going on out there. In fact, it almost sounded like our school cafeteria sounds when the lunchroom monitor steps outside for a few minutes. There was so much racket that I could hardly even hear the piano player pounding out a bouncy tune in the background.

"Sorry I'm late, Wilbur," I said. I glanced around quickly, still hoping to spot the stuffed rattlesnake—

but no such luck. I considered just making a dive for Hooten, hoping to catch him by surprise, but decided against it. Although his guns were still holstered, I had a feeling he could get them out real quick if he needed to.

Wilbur was casting curious glances at Hooten, who was busy arranging his cape, adjusting his holsters on his hips, and practicing his squinty-eyed look.

Suddenly, from the other side of the curtain came a cry of "YA-HOOOOOOO!" followed by a chorus of whistles and cheers. And then Nellie's outraged voice roared, "You git yerself down from there, Clem! That there chandelier come all the way from St. Louis!"

Hooten looked at me a little nervously. "Is the crowd always this rambunctious?" he asked.

"Are you kidding?" I said. "This is nothing. They're just getting warmed up. Wait'll the curtain goes up, and then they'll *really* be ready to romp. They can hog-tie a man, haul him outside, and dump him in a horse trough in about six seconds flat. You want to call it off?"

The audience had begun stomping their feet in unison and chanting, "LANGSFIELD! LANGSFIELD! LANGSFIELD!" The chant grew louder and louder, until the walls shook.

Hooten hesitated, chewing his lip. For a moment there I thought he was going to chicken out. But no. The lure of fame was too strong.

"Nope," he said firmly. "We come this far, let's git on with it. You go on out there and introduce me. And, Langsfield," he warned, narrowing his eyes, *"make it good."*

"Introduce *you?*" piped up Wilbur, looking puzzled. "Who're you?"

"You'll find out soon enough," said Hooten with a grim smile. "Meanwhile, bub, you kin git over there and git ready to pull that curtain rope."

Wilbur drew himself up. *"Bub?"* he said indignantly. "Did I understand you to say 'bub'? Sir, I am not accustomed to being addressed as 'bub.' My name is Wilbur J. McNabb, *the* Wilbur J. McNabb, and as people say about me all the way from Montana to Texas, I am—"

*"Now,"* barked Hooten. He rested his hand meaningfully on his gun.

"On my way," said Wilbur, hurrying toward the curtain rope.

Slowly and uncertainly, I walked to the center of the stage and faced the curtain. Was I actually going to do this? I asked myself. Was I actually going to introduce Hooten so he could rob everybody?

The palms of my hands had begun to sweat. My knees felt wobbly.

The worst part, I thought to myself, was the effect this was going to have on Desmond Langsfield—the *real* Desmond Langsfield. I mean, suppose I did survive until the next day when the time machine was scheduled to whisk Max and me back to the present. How was Desmond Langsfield going to feel when he took over his body again and found out that he'd made a complete idiot of himself as an undercover detective? Not only had he been captured by the very outlaws he'd been hired to catch, but he'd even helped them rob the entire town. It didn't take a genius to figure out that all this wasn't going to look very good on his work record. He'd probably be drummed right out of the undercover detective business. In fact, after this, he'd be lucky if he could get a job reloading Junior Sitwell's peashooter.

Hooten gave the signal and Wilbur started pulling on the rope, hand over hand. The curtain rose. The piano stopped playing and the audience broke into cheers.

Boy, it was a packed house, all right. Every available space was filled with someone sitting, standing, or trying to steal someone else's place.

There was Max. Standing near the front door. And there was the Tumbleweed Kid, standing almost behind him, one hand hidden inside his coat and the other clamped on Max's shoulder.

Max stared at me with dismay. Of course, as soon as he saw me up there on the stage, he knew what it meant: Operation Conk had fizzled. And his stunned expression said that he didn't have any brilliant last-minute ideas for what to do about it.

I spotted Nellie standing a few feet away from Max. She had her thumbs hooked in her suspenders and was beaming at me proudly. As soon as she caught my eye, she grinned and gave me a hearty good-luck wave.

I smiled back feebly. Sure, she liked me now, but how was she going to feel after I'd helped Hooten collect all those lockets from everybody's pockets?

The audience had quieted down. Uh-oh, this was it. Hundreds of eyes were on me. The air vibrated with excitement. I tried to swallow, but my mouth was too dry.

"Ladies and gentlemen!" I managed to say.

It came out sort of squeaky.

I cleared my throat, coughed nervously, took a deep breath, and tried again. "Ladies and gentlemen!" I boomed.

That was better.

I glanced offstage at Hooten. He was peering out at the audience, looking about as nervous as I was. More nervous, maybe. In fact, he looked like he wished he were somewhere else, doing something nice and safe—like robbing a stagecoach.

And that's when I got an idea.

It wasn't the best idea I'd ever had, but it wasn't the worst, either. It was definitely worth a try.

"Ladies and gentlemen!" I boomed again. "Hang on to your seats! It is my pleasure to inform you that you have another special treat in store for you tonight!"

I paused for a few seconds, letting the suspense build, and then went on.

"It just so happens that we have with us here one of the West's most colorful and delightful characters. He will have some rather important business to transact with you in a few minutes, but before then I have asked him to entertain you with one or two jokes. One or two *hilarious* jokes. If this man can't make you laugh, well, then, you'd better check your pulse to see if you're still alive! He is not a professional comedian, but he is, in my humble opinion, an extremely talented man and one heck of a funny guy. Come on out here, John! Give him a big hand, folks!"

Just as I knew they would, the audience burst into a storm of applause.

126

From the wings, Gentleman John Hooten looked at me in astonishment. Then he looked down at his guns, which he had already drawn in preparation for his grand entrance. Then he peeked cautiously around the edge of the stage at the audience. He was tempted, all right. That applause was music to his ears. I could almost hear his mind working: *Well, maybe just one or two little jokes before I rob 'em.*

Slowly he slipped his guns back into his holsters. Nervously he straightened his fur-trimmed cape. Then he took a deep breath and walked stiffly out onto the stage—looking sideways at the audience, a weak grin on his face.

I stepped aside and let him take the center of the stage.

A few people in the audience were staring at Hooten in surprise, their hands frozen in mid-clap. I figured they must've recognized the Rhyming Robber of the Rockies. But most of the crowd obviously didn't know who he was, because they just kept on applauding and cheering as he walked onstage, and then quieted down and sat there, waiting for him to speak.

"Er, ahem. Howdy, folks," said Hooten, giving a little wave. The audience waited in silence. Beads of sweat broke out on Hooten's forehead.

"Uh, well . . ." he said, coughing into his hand. He shifted his weight uneasily. "Well, see, there was this grizzly bear, once. And he had this friend that was a horse, and he had this other friend that was a duck." He paused, shifting his weight again and laughing nervously. "Heh, heh."

"That's it?" came a loud voice from the front row. "That's yer joke? Heck, that ain't funny!"

It was Mountain MacLachlan, sitting right there at front row center, glowering up at Hooten from under his bushy black eyebrows.

"Well, a'*course* it ain't funny!" exploded Hooten. "I ain't hardly started yet, you blockhead!"

Mountain threw off his buffalo robe and stood up—all six-and-a-half, hulking, muscular, buckskin-clad feet of him.

"Ain't *nobody* gonna call *me* a blockhead," he growled, starting for the stage.

Hooten's eyes went wide. "Uh-oh," I heard him say under his breath.

*"Fight!"* yelled a bunch of people at once.

As Mountain climbed onto the stage and started for Hooten, fights broke out all over the theater. This was just what I'd been hoping for. A little good, healthy confusion. I moved fast.

Mountain was almost on top of Hooten. Hooten went for his guns!

But they were no longer in his holsters.

I'd moved in from behind and drawn them already.

Hooten's hands hit empty leather. "Ulp!" he said, just as Mountain reached out with his huge, hairy hands and grabbed him by the front of the shirt.

Figuring that Hooten was in safe hands, I leaped out of the way and looked over the heads of the brawling crowd for Max. The first thing my eyes focused on was the Tumbleweed Kid, whipping his gun out from under his coat and aiming it across the theater at me, his arm extended. At the same instant—with a terrific "HAIII-YA!"—Max brought his arm down hard across the Tumbleweed Kid's wrist. The gun clattered to the floor.

Nellie whirled around. "You brung a *gun* in here?" she bellowed, outraged. She seemed to know exactly what to do. Stepping forward, she decked the Tumbleweed Kid with a powerful uppercut to the jaw.

So much for the Tumbleweed Kid. I glanced around. Mountain MacLachlan was sitting on top of Hooten. So much for Hooten.

Meanwhile, six or seven other fights were going strong all over the theater. Across the sea of crashing chairs and flying fists, I caught Max's eye—and we exchanged triumphant grins. We'd done it! We'd actually captured the bad guys!

Just then Sheriff Parker burst through the front door. He took one look around, drew his gun, and fired three shots into the ceiling.

The citizens of Silver Gulch broke it up fast and began tumbling out the door and windows.

Suddenly, Wilbur appeared at my side. "Need any help, Mr. Langsfield?" he asked brightly, vigorously dusting off his knees.

It looked like he'd been spending some time under a table somewhere.

# 21

"Your card," said Max briskly, "is the eight of diamonds."

It was the next morning, shortly before the time machine was due to bring us back to the present, and Max and I were having breakfast with Nellie and Sheriff Parker at Ma Peterson's Restaurant and Chop House. It was a late breakfast because it had taken a couple of hours just to walk over from the hotel. Every ten paces or so, Max and I had been hailed by someone who wanted to shake our hands, or whack us on our backs, or just generally tell us how great we were for having captured Gentleman John Hooten and the Tumbleweed Kid.

"Why, danged if you ain't right, Mr. Huff!" exclaimed Nellie, looking at her card, astonished. "It *is* the eight of diamonds! How'd you do that?"

"Sorry," said Max, shuffling the cards. "A magician never gives away his secrets." He fanned out the cards again. "Pick a card, Nellie, any card."

The sheriff took that opportunity to lean over to me.

"Langsfield," he said in a low voice, "I telegraphed Pink Elephant this morning and told him that the ducks are in the soup."

Unless I missed my guess, the sheriff was talking in code again. I gathered he meant that he'd sent a telegram to the Pinkerton National Detective Agency and told them that Hooten and the Tumbleweed Kid were behind bars.

"I told Pink Elephant there wouldn't be any more quacking around here," added the sheriff.

I nodded. "I reckon they've quacked their last quack, all right."

"I've never seen a slicker piece of work, Langsfield," said Sheriff Parker. His keen gray eyes were full of admiration. "It's been a privilege working with you."

"Thanks, sheriff," I whispered. "Of course, I had a lot of help. I mean—"

"The ace of hearts!" declared Max.

"Well, I'll be a—" began Nellie.

"And that very ace of hearts is now located. . . " Max continued dramatically, with his eyes closed and his fingertips pressed against his forehead, ". . . *under that plate!*" He pointed to an empty serving plate in the middle of the table.

Nellie grabbed up the plate. There on the table was the ace of hearts.

"If that don't beat all!" she burst out, staring at Max.

Max grinned. "It was nothing," he said modestly

as he set the cards aside. He helped himself to some more beans and bacon.

Nellie gulped down the last of her coffee and stood up.

"Well, I'd best be gittin' back to the theater," she said. She grinned down at me. "I know you ain't had a chance to do yer show yet, Mr. Langsfield, but tonight's finally gonna be the night. And jest wait'll you see the size of yer audience! After what you done last night, *ever'body's* gonna be there. Folks is even comin' all the way from Mule Junction and Harrisville jest to see yer show. Why, this here performance is shapin' up to be the biggest doggone cultur'l event Silver Gulch has ever seen!"

"Desmond Langsfield won't let them down," I assured her.

Meaning, of course, the *real* Desmond Langsfield, since Max and I were going to be winging back to the present in—I glanced at my pocket watch— about five minutes.

"Well," said Nellie, "I gotta git movin'. See you gents later." She slapped her hat on her head and strode out the door.

"A fine woman, that Nellie Bradshaw," said the sheriff, buttering a biscuit.

"You bet," Max and I said together.

I started to reach for the pitcher of milk, but suddenly out of the corner of my eye, I saw a suspicious movement. Something in the open doorway. Without moving my head, I glanced quickly over.

It was Junior! That little rat, Junior Sitwell. And he was taking aim at me with his peashooter!

I ducked.

Just in time.

SPLAT! A large, wet spitball struck the sheriff on the side of his nose.

Sheriff Parker spun around with his eyes narrowed fiercely.

Junior's face froze in mid-snicker as he realized with horror what he'd just done. Slowly the sheriff peeled the spitball off his nose, studied it grimly, and then looked back at Junior. Junior tried an innocent grin but it came out weak and guilty.

Sheriff Parker slowly pushed back his chair and stood up. "You men will excuse me," he said with quiet determination. "I have me some business to attend to."

With wide eyes and a gulp, Junior lurched away from the door, making a break for it. Sheriff Parker started for the door, taking long, businesslike strides.

"Oh, sheriff," I called after him helpfully. "Junior's pretty fast on his feet. I think I'd hurry if I were you."

"Right," said the sheriff, breaking into a trot. He disappeared through the door, and we heard his boots pounding down the boardwalk.

Max and I looked at each other, both of us trying to keep a straight face.

"What do you reckon, stranger?" Max drawled. "You reckon Junior'll hang up his peashooter and go straight?"

"I reckon so," I drawled. "What's left of him."

We broke out laughing. And, jumping up, we ran toward the door, hoping to catch a glimpse of Sheriff Parker closing in on Junior.

But we never made it.

133

We hadn't gone more than four steps before the inside of Ma Peterson's restaurant suddenly dissolved into nothingness, and in its place were a thousand dancing, swirling, sparkling lights. A tremendous two-hundred-mile-an-hour wind struck us in the face—and we were swept away.

Professor Flybender's Fully Guaranteed One-Of-A-Kind Time Machine was doing its stuff.

# 22

"Come on, Max," I said. "What're you worried about? You're going to be great! Trust me."

Max and I were standing under the streetlight in front of Dawn Sharington's house. Max was wearing the black cape and top hat he'd borrowed, and was carrying a large cardboard box full of magic equipment.

Max the Magnificent was having some last-minute doubts about his upcoming show.

"I'm going to blow it. I know I'm going to blow it. I've never given a magic show in my life! What if I can't escape from the Impossible Knot? What if the Floating Pencil won't float? The entire girls' softball team is in there. They'll laugh me right out of the house!" He looked at me sternly. "Of course, if a certain somebody hadn't volunteered me, I wouldn't be in this pickle."

What Max needed was a little pep talk, and I was just the guy to give it to him.

"Look, Max," I said firmly. "You've got to have

a little confidence in yourself. I mean, you practiced your magic tricks while we were in the Wild West, didn't you? And you've practiced all afternoon since we got back, haven't you? With no mistakes, right? So what's there to worry about?"

I paused. Max looked skeptical, but he was listening. I went on.

"Now, I know what you're thinking, Max. You're thinking Dawn's in there. The girl of your dreams. But so what? What's the worst that can happen? I mean, suppose you bomb. Suppose you bomb *bad*. Suppose Dawn and the other girls *do* laugh you right out of the house. So? I mean, sure she's got electric-blue eyes. Sure she's got a great smile. Sure you're head-over-heels in love with her. But why take it so hard? There'll be other girls. Someday. See what I mean? Relax and enjoy yourself, Max. Learn from your mistakes."

Max glared at me. "Was that a pep talk?" he demanded.

"Yes, it was."

"Is it over?"

"Yes, it is."

"Good. I'm not certain, but I think I may have survived it."

We started up the walk toward the door. It was hard to tell in that light, but I was pretty sure Max's ears had turned pink. The mere mention of Dawn's name tends to have that effect on him.

"Don't you just love show business?" I asked cheerfully. "The excitement, the thrills, the cheering crowds." I sighed loudly. "You know, Max, I don't mind telling you that I already miss being Desmond

Langsfield. Just think, I was a real, live actor! And a famous, talented, incredibly handsome actor, too, I might add."

I cracked my knuckles.

"Oh, that reminds me," said Max, stopping suddenly and putting down his box. "I forgot to give you your hat and your guns."

"Huh?" I said. "What hat? What guns?"

He bent over, opened the top of the box, and began fishing around inside. "They're here somewhere," he said.

"Max, *what* hat? *What* guns?"

"Your cowboy hat and your six-guns," he said briskly. He stood up and handed me a large cowboy hat and a couple of plastic six-shooters. "I borrowed these this afternoon. It's your Frankie LaRue costume. After the magic show's over, I'm going to introduce you so you can do your play, *A Ghost! A Ghost! I See a Ghost!*"

"You *what?* You're going to *what?*"

"After all, Steve," he said, "you never got a chance to perform in the Wild West, so I thought I'd give you your chance tonight. It's only fair."

He picked up the box and started toward the door again. I charged after him, sputtering, "Max, you can't—"

"Don't thank me now," he said cheerfully, going up the front steps and ringing the doorbell. "Just relax and enjoy yourself."

"Max, the whole girls' softball team is in there! I'm not even sure I can remember my lines. And look at this hat! It's—"

The door opened.

"Hi, Mrs. Sharington," said Max.

"Well, right on time!" she said, smiling. "You must be Max the Magnificent and his assistant, Steve the Stupendous."

"At your service," said Max.

*Wolves!* I said to myself, concentrating like crazy. *Maybe twenty of 'em. Traveling in a—*

"You have no idea how excited the girls are about your show," Mrs. Sharington was saying. "Dawn hasn't talked about anything else all day!"

"Oh?" Max gulped.

Girls' voices—lots of them—came drifting out from somewhere inside.

*Traveling in a pack—and hungry! I oughta build a fire, but . . . but . . . but . . .* But what? I racked my memory. But *what?*

"Just follow me," said Mrs. Sharington, starting down the hall.

"Right," said Max, following her.

*I oughta build a fire, but . . . but . . . but . . .*

I hurried after them.

"Max, wait!"